THIRD CHANCES

A LUCA MYSTERY
BOOK 4

DAN PETROSINI

Print ISBN: 978-1-960286-06-2
Naples, FL
Library of Congress Control Number: 2023901520

OTHER BOOKS BY DAN

Complicit Witness

Push Back

Ambition Cliff

ACKNOWLEDGMENTS

Special thanks to Julie, Stephanie and Jennifer for their love and support, and thanks to Squad Sergeant Craig Perrilli for his counsel on the real world of law enforcement. He helps me keep it real.

1

―――――

IT WAS 8:07 WHEN I PULLED UP TO JOEY CHAPMAN'S apartment off Goodlette. A light drizzle intensified as Joey trotted to my car. The timing was perfect. The Dark Sky app said heavy rain would hit around 8:22. God was truly in control.

Joey jumped in, brushing the rain out of his hair. "It's gonna come down."

I pulled away. "You can set your watch to the summer rain."

"Whaddaya need help with?"

"You'll see when we get there."

"What are you, all full of mysterious shit?"

"A friend from church is down-and-out. That's all."

Joey reached for the radio. "What the hell you listening to? It's like elevator shit."

Passing under 75, heading east as Chapman hunted for a country music station, I kept thinking, who's going to elimi-nate evil sinners, if not me? They've had opportunities for redemption and blown them all. They're irredeemable.

I snaked off and on Collier Boulevard, back to Golden

Gate, making small talk. Approaching Wilson Boulevard, I said, "The devil has a hold on you, Joey."

"What the fuck you talking about?"

"When The Spirit of Fellowship took you in, you promised you'd get right with God. But it's one thing after another with you."

"Hey, I'm trying to change. It ain't so easy."

"You're hopeless, you're not interested in changing."

"Bullshit. I'm making progress."

The windshield wipers couldn't keep up with the volume of water, so I slowed down.

"We've got different definitions of progress, Joey. You robbed that convenience store in Bonita and put that poor man into a coma."

"No way. I had nothing to do with that."

I shook my head. "Lying only compounds your sin, Joseph."

"I swear to God, it wasn't me."

"Look at you. Now you're taking the name of God in vain."

"I'm just saying it wasn't me."

"Larry told me you asked him to commit the crime with him."

"He's a fucking rat."

I checked the rearview mirror—not a car in sight—and pulled over.

"Why you stopping here for?"

"You're getting out."

"What, are you kidding me? in this rain?"

Hand trembling, I reached under my thigh. Ignoring my back pain, I pulled a Colt .45 automatic out. "Get out. Now!"

"You fucking kidding me? You grow balls or something?"

"Out!"

As Chapman got out, he said, "You're fucking crazy, you know that?"

Sliding into the passenger seat, I opened the window. "Step away from the car."

He took two steps back, and I fired two bullets into the heathen's chest. Chapman collapsed into the gully, sending a splash into the air. I looked left and right—was he dead? It was tough to see if he was breathing, with all the rain. Opening the door, I hung on to the steering wheel and leaned out. Chapman was facedown, water covering his ears. He couldn't be breathing.

A smile erupted on my face. Pride coursed through my body. It felt unbelievable being God's avenger, exactly as Romans 13:4 said, 'I was God's servant, an avenger carrying out God's wrath on wrongdoers.'

We were in a battle with evil to the end, and I was finally a warrior for the Lord.

I was tired of all the talking, begging people to change. It was the same worthless plea made for centuries. History proved people don't change when the devil gets a hold of them. Once Satan corrupts them, they're beyond saving.

I knew God would protect me as I carried out his work, but I had to be smart about it, lest I be taken off the battlefield.

2

———————

GRAYNESS BATTLED THE SUN FOR SUPREMACY ON THE morning of June twenty-fifth. It was only 8:10. By nine, the sun would prevail, as it always did. Pulling behind three police cars with blazing lights, I took a long look around. It was as close to desolate as you could get fifteen minutes from Golden Gate. Was time an issue for whoever did this?

The responding officers had restricted traffic to a single lane on the opposite side of the road from where the body lay. It wasn't enough. I shouted an order to have the road completely closed. Who knew what we'd find combing both sides of the roadway?

As two patrol cars maneuvered into blocking positions, I approached the body. A Caucasian male, medium build with dark hair, lay sprawled headfirst in a drainage gully. A thin, black jacket was scrunched up, revealing a white tee shirt and a hint of a tattoo. Plant particles and dirt were scattered on his shoulders and hair, unfortunate evidence that water had rushed over him.

Pulling on gloves and booties, I stepped into the muddy gully. The corpse's face lay on its right cheek, and his left eye looked hazed over. Bending over, a chill shot up my spine as a red ant crawled out of his nose. I took note of a thin scar on his forehead before reaching into the back pockets of his worn jeans.

A cheap wallet, which I bagged, was in the left pocket and a phone in the right. The phone wouldn't turn on. I couldn't tell if it was the battery or if it had shorted from getting wet and dropped it into another bag. Either way, the lab would get me the contacts and usage information.

It took two of us to roll the body over. He looked to be in his mid-thirties. Caked with mud, the victim's right eye was open, no doubt dead when he collapsed. His white tee shirt was reddish brown, partially masking two entrance wounds, one in the left pectoral area and the other, dead center, below the rib cage. I wanted to check the front pockets, but they were caked with dirt. I wouldn't risk losing any forensic evidence. We eased the body back to its original position as the CSI van pulled up.

A pair of crime scene investigators I'd worked with, more than I cared to recall, approached. I told them how I handled the body, and left, hoping they'd give me something to work with. As four of the uniformed officers began a grid search for evidence, including bullet shells, I took out the wallet.

According to the driver's license, the victim was Joseph L. Chapman. Residing on 104th Street, the thirty-six-year-old was five eight and a hundred and fifty-five pounds. The wallet was stuffed with twenty-dollar bills and contained a Visa debit card and two pictures that were impossible to decipher. After bagging it, I called Vargas, asking her to look into Chapman.

Vargas gave me a warm smile when I got to the office.

"Looks like you need some coffee, Frank. I'll get you a cup."

"It's okay, I'll get my own. What'd you get on Chapman?"

"You'd better grab a coffee. This guy has a long history, and none of it's good."

Moving close to Vargas's desk, I caught a whiff of her candy-like perfume. "Let's hear it."

"Chapman spent half his life behind bars. Break-ins, a handful of armed robberies, and two nasty assaults are the highlights. He wasn't on the outside long. Chapman just got out of Immokalee seven months ago."

"Parole?"

Vargas nodded. "Shiler was his parole officer. Third time he had him."

I slumped into a chair. "We've got to waste time chasing this down? Whoever killed him did us a favor."

"Really?"

"I'm just saying, this Chapman was a punk, and we've got to waste resources on finding who finally stopped him?"

"So, you'd rather do nothing and let some vigilante mete out justice?"

I frowned. "I was hoping we could bury this somehow. You know I need to take some time off to find a place to live."

"I told you, the cabana is all yours."

It was perfect, but Vargas and I had just started dating. We'd had three dates, and things were going well. Even though the cabana was separate, we'd know each other's comings and goings, and it didn't feel right.

"Believe me, it'd make things a helluva a lot easier and

take the pressure off, but I don't want to, you know, screw things up between us."

"Come on, Frank, we're adults."

Maybe one of us was. I lowered my voice. "But I really want this to work with us."

"That's sweet, Frank. I understand. Whatever you're comfortable with is good by me."

3

———————

AFTER READING THE TITLE OF AN EMAIL, I SAID, "HEY, Vargas, the autopsy on Chapman came in."

"Anything?" Vargas came around my desk. Her honeysuckle perfume sure smelled good. It was the same one Kayla used to wear. She was something, someone who I thought would work out for me. I wondered if she was with anybody and whether I should risk calling her when Vargas said,

"Hello? You there, Frank?"

"Yeah, yeah. The bullets were hollow points. Whoever it was wasn't taking any chances Chapman would survive. Maybe there was something, a secret of some kind, the killer wanted to die with Chapman."

"They never found any shells at the scene, right?"

"Nothing. The killer picked them up."

"Maybe, but I was thinking, what if he or she shot this guy from a car or truck. The shells could've ended up in the car."

I really liked Vargas, she was a good detective, but I was getting tired of her coming up with scenarios that I used to spit out. Losing my bladder to cancer wasn't enough? The chemo had to take my memory?

"I was thinking the same thing. When we track this down, we'll have to look for any burn markings the casings might have left."

"Besides the hollow point info, there's nothing but a time of death of around nine p.m."

"Forensics discover anything?"

"Nada. Said the rain could've washed away any fibers or hairs," Vargas replied, adding, "Let's start with the victim's mother."

I had zero interest wasting time on a small-time thug, but I wasn't gonna say anything and be labeled insensitive.

CHAPMAN'S MOTHER lived in one of a series of yellow cinder-block units off Terry Street in Bonita. Vargas and I were greeted by loud Mexican music that was spilling out of the open windows in the next apartment. No air-conditioning? In late June?

Anita Chapman, a bird of a woman, showed us in. There was a galley kitchen and a bedroom beyond the living room. It was tiny but clean and it had a window AC unit humming away. There was a smell of something that'd been baked. If nothing else, maybe we'd get a cookie out of the visit.

Vargas said, "Please accept our condolences, ma'am. We know how difficult this must be, but we need your help and have some questions for you."

"It's a parent's worst nightmare to have your child die before you do."

I swallowed hard, pulling out my notebook.

Vargas said, "We're sorry."

"Joseph wasn't an easy child, but I can tell you, it doesn't make it any easier."

Her lips quivered, and Vargas rubbed her back.

"Why don't we sit down?"

My stomach reacted to a plate of cookies on the counter. Eyes on the dish, I pulled a chair away from the kitchen table, and Chapman's mother sat.

"Mrs. Chapman, we need your help with some background on your son."

Vargas glared at me and said, "If you're ready to talk. Can I get you a drink of water?"

She nodded. "Thanks. I'm okay, what do you want to know?"

Vargas asked, "When was the last time you saw your son?"

"Day before yesterday. He came to see me, said he was doing good, even paid back some money he'd borrowed."

I said, "Mind if we ask how much?"

"Five hundred dollars."

I said, "That's a lot of money. You know where he got it?"

"I stopped asking a long time ago. Look, my son was no angel, but he seemed to be doing good." Her voice took on a vibrato quality. "He had a tough time growing up."

"He was bullied?"

She nodded. "Joey was different, and everybody knows that kids can be mean."

Amen to that. Even this detective gets embarrassed when he recalls the taunting he took part in.

I said, "What about his friends? Anything you can tell us? Was there anyone new?"

"He was mostly a loner. I mean he had some friends and all, but he kinda bounced around."

I said, "Joseph had been in a lot of trouble with the law

over the years. Most people like him tend to hang around with the same crowd."

"I never liked the people he ran around with, and I told him so. But I was talking to myself. I don't know. What he really needed was a father around to straighten him out."

Vargas reached across the table and patted her hand. "I'm sure you did the best you could."

"But you know, it's funny, maybe he was listening after all, because the other day he said he was leaving to meet a friend from church."

I felt bad for this lady. Who knew if she was a good mother or not? End of the day, her kid was lying on a stainless-steel tray in the county morgue.

Vargas asked, "Is there anyone you could think of that could do something like this to Joseph?"

She shook her head. "No, I can't imagine anything like that. Maybe you should check with Paulie Lenin. Joseph and he used to be close."

We asked a few more questions, said our goodbyes, and headed for the car without a cookie.

Pulling away from the curb, I said, "That was a complete waste of time, time I don't have."

"We know he was flush with cash."

"You ask me, Chapman pulled a job, and whoever he did it with offed him."

"Maybe he stole from the wrong people. A narcotics dealer or something."

Another angle I should have thought of. "Could be, but they did us a favor."

Phone in hand, Vargas exhaled. "You know, Frank, sometimes you can be an ass."

"Just sometimes?"

Vargas, phone to ear, shook her head as she tracked down where Paul Lenin lived.

APPROPRIATELY NAMED, Moss Wood Road had a collection of wood-framed houses, horseshoed around a gravel driveway. The homes were checkered with plywood patches and blue tarps on the roofs. These places would be destroyed in the next hurricane, if the big bad wolf didn't come by first.

Pulling up, a flash of red caught my eye. A guy in a tee shirt was walking away from Lenin's place carrying two red bottles of Tide.

"There he is." Vargas pointed to a covered car park framed by a pair of spindly palm trees.

Loud rap music, now that's an oxymoron. rap and music in the same sentence, assaulted us as we approached. A tall man with a shaved head and a beard was on a stool next to a folding table.

"Paul Lenin?"

"Yeah, you cops?"

I hadn't yet pulled my badge, but the criminal element had a sixth sense when it came to law enforcement. Their problem was it didn't extend past recognition.

I stuck my badge out. Scanning the table, I saw hooks, metal fish, and colored strings. "You making lures?"

"Yeah, you fish?"

"No, but my dad used to go out every now and then."

"You should get into it; it's very relaxing."

"Maybe I will. We wanted to ask you about Joseph Chapman."

"I don't know anything."

"You know what happened to Chapman?"

He nodded.

Vargas said, "When was the last time you saw him?"

Lenin's eyes moved from her face to mine. "I had nothing to do with that. Me and Joe were friends."

"She's not saying you did. Her question was about the last time you saw him."

He hesitated. "A couple of days ago."

Lenin had a record but had stayed out of trouble or hadn't been caught over the last two years. I said, "If you had nothing to do with his death, you don't have to worry. We're looking for information to solve his murder. Anything you tell us won't go anywhere."

"I don't know anything."

Vargas said, "You two were friends. What was Chapman up to that could have gotten him killed?"

Lenin picked up a hook and was gently tapping a thumb on the sharp end of it.

"You've got nothing to fear. Detective Luca already told you any information you provide will stay with us."

"Joey was Joey. He didn't say much. We didn't see each other too much anymore. We were out of touch."

I made like I was looking at the array of fishing gear and sneaked a look in the window. There were four rows of boxes, stacked three high, emblazoned with the Tide logo. I wouldn't need any sodium thiopental to crack this criminal clam open.

"Cut the crap, we don't have time. You don't start talking, I'm gonna get a subpoena and turn your place upside down."

Vargas's eyes widened, and I said, "Either this guy has a fetish about washing his clothes, or we found some of the stuff from the trailer that was hijacked out of Walmart's distribution center."

"It wasn't me. I swear."

Oh, if he's swearing, it's got to be true. "Look, I told you up front, I'm not looking to bust you. I want information. You talk, and I chalk you up as a clean-clothes nut."

Vargas said, "Tell us what you know."

Lenin clamped his eyes shut for a second and then spewed. "He came to me about a couple of jobs he wanted to pull. I told him I don't do anything like that anymore. I mean it, I don't. I steer clear of that. I ain't going back in."

"Jobs? He was planning robberies?"

He nodded.

"You know if he did them?"

He nodded. "It was in the papers. He robbed the 7-Eleven off Golden Gate. At least I think it was him."

We'd have to check the CCTV video. "He wanted you to do the 7-Eleven with him?"

"Yeah, that one, and a gas station convenience store on Airport."

"The Chevron station?"

"Yeah, that's the one he said."

Lenin didn't give us anything else, but as far as I was concerned it was enough. Plus, if we could tie Chapman to the robberies with the video feeds, we'd solve two crimes. Chapman was a cretin, and I didn't want to waste any more time tracking down his killer, who probably settled a dispute with a gun. I'd have to find a way to let this case fade away.

4

THE WESTERN SIDE OF THE SKY WAS CHARCOAL GRAY AND THE morning air cool as we crossed the police line on Vanderbilt Drive. I scanned the area from the southern tip of the Coco-hatchee River Park to Island Marina. The water was moving westward to the Gulf of Mexico.

A jet ski laden with two onlookers came into view. It slowed to an idle as it approached. How did people find out so soon?

Vargas asked the responding officer, "Who found the body?"

"Guy was going fishing and saw him floating over there." He pointed toward a small alcove. "Took his boat over to see what was going on and called it in."

"He touch anything?"

"He prodded him with the back of his gaffe to see if there was any movement. Then he dragged the body into the mouth of the marina."

We bounced down an aluminum gangway onto the Trex docking toward the strobe lights. A photographer was documenting the scene, and it was a tough crime scene. There were an endless number of places the body could have entered the water. Was it off a boat deep in the bay and the current carried it, or was it dumped off land?

A small tropical depression had passed through yesterday, bringing heavy rain and unfavorable marine conditions. How long was the body in the water? There were a lot of questions needing answers.

Bobbing gently, the body was pressed against the bow of a police boat. Bracing myself with a piling, I leaned toward the body. Faceup, it was a male in his thirties dressed in jeans and a black shirt. There were at least two gunshot wounds, one in his right chest and another in the gut.

There was limited bloating and no deterioration. It was likely the body was in the water well under a day. Pocketing the first answer, I ordered the police boat to fish the corpse out and turned to Vargas.

"Let's see if he's carrying any ID."

"You think he was killed elsewhere and dumped?"

"That'd depend on who he is. If he owns a boat or goes fishing, he could've been shot on the water, where there's a helluva lot less witnesses."

"Chapman also took two shots to the chest."

"Tough to forget that one, even if he deserved it."

Vargas glared at me and turned away.

"Hold on, Mary Ann, I'm just kidding." I wasn't, but we had a date tomorrow, and I might need her cabana to live in.

WATER LACED with seaweed draped off the body as it was lifted out of the bay. I made a note that the corpse was dropped onto the tarp-covered dock, too heavily for my taste. The body's feet were bare. Was that a sign he'd been on a boat? Or was he wearing flip-flops when he met his maker?

Pulling on gloves, I bent over the body. There were only two wounds I could see.

"Vargas, let's put him on his side."

I lifted his upper torso as Vargas twisted his hips. There looked to be at least one exit wound. Vargas dug into the back pockets, fishing out a wallet and phone. We eased the body back, instructing the officers it was okay to wrap the body for transport to the coroner.

The cheap wallet frayed as Vargas opened it.

"Be careful. Just see if there's a license and leave the rest for the lab."

Vargas slid out a laminated license, examined it quickly, and handed it to me as she bagged the wallet.

Checking the picture against the corpse, it was clearly a match. His name was Brett Tinder, and he lived on Radio Road. I took a picture of the license and dropped it in the bag with the wallet.

As soon as I got to our office, Vargas said, "Tinder's got a rap sheet."

"What offenses?"

"He's no Chapman, but two burglaries and a pair of domestic violences."

"He's married?"

"Don't think so, but he's got a temper. The complaints were from different women."

"Frigging coward. Maybe it was a girlfriend who got sick of being abused by the piece of shit."

"You know that's not likely, Frank."

"I know. Still, we'll need to talk with them."

"You want to start with them or his mother?"

"Has she been notified?"

"Yeah, Alvarez went."

"Good, let's start with whoever's closer."

"The mother lives in Leigh Acres—both women in East Naples."

"East Naples, here we come."

"Okay. I also sent a car out to his neighborhood—see what they come up with contact wise."

"Good move. Let's get going."

As Vargas holstered her gun she said, "I asked the lab to run ballistics on the bullets used on Chapman and Tinder. It's an outside shot they're connected, but we got two bodies in just under two weeks."

She was good. As a nonbeliever in conspiracies, I didn't see the connection, but it was the right move. If we had a serial killer on our hands who was wiping out thugs, I was of the opinion we either drag our feet or add them to the force.

5

———

I COULDN'T EVEN PUT A VALUE ON A PLACE LIKE THE ONE Tinder's girlfriend lived in. The cinder-block home was missing roof tiles, and a piece of graying plywood covered a window. The front yard of Jean Baron's home was littered with plastic furniture and bicycles in various states of disrepair. I rang the bell with my car key.

Jean Baron had a drinker's nose and was still in a housecoat, though it was near noon. Her eyes were red. Either she'd been nipping a bottle, or she knew about Tinder. I could hear one of those stupid courtroom shows playing on a TV.

Vargas said, "Jean Baron?"

Baron nodded slowly.

"We're detectives Vargas and Luca from the sheriff's department."

"You're here about Brett, right?"

Vargas nodded. "You know what happened to him?"

She nodded. "His mother called me."

"May we come in?"

Baron moved to the side, and we stepped into a small

family room with a flat-screen TV so big it overpowered the room. The place smelled of fried chicken.

"Can I get you anything?"

"No thanks. We'd like to ask you some questions about Mr. Tinder to get some background as to how this could have happened."

"It was inevitable."

I asked, "What do you mean by that?"

"I mean Brett had some good parts of him. He was good with my kids, and he didn't have to be. He treated them like his own. It was the only reason I stuck with him."

"How long were you with him?"

"Off and on about six years."

"Why'd you leave him?"

"Come on, you know damn well. I filed against him. He beat the hell out of me in front of the kids."

"Was that the first time he laid a hand on you?"

She shook her head. "Like I said, I hung around for the kids."

I said, "You said his mother called you. Are the two of you close?"

"Emily's a saint. She ain't got nobody but Brett, and he was always in trouble. I felt for her."

"What did Mr. Tinder do for a living?"

She snorted. "You mean besides stealing and dealing?"

I stole a glance at Vargas before asking, "He dealt drugs?"

"Nothing big, but I caught him with a big bag of pills one day. That's the first time I threw him out. He begged to come back, and like a fool I took him in. But he kept his word on that at least, because I never saw any drugs, and believe me, with two kids, I looked."

I asked, "Did he know someone named Joe Chapman?"

"Chapman? No, I don't think so."

Vargas handed her a photo of Chapman.

"I ain't never seen this guy before."

Vargas took back the picture and asked, "You said Mr. Tinder was always in trouble. What do you mean by that?"

"Really? You guys arrested him and sent him to prison, didn't you?"

"Detective Vargas was looking for information unrelated to his record. Things he may have gotten away with."

"Brett was a thief, inside and out. He would steal something almost everywhere we went, like it was a game."

"Did he have anyone you'd consider an enemy?"

"He'd get into fights, come home all bruised up. But it's been a good two years since we've been together, and I don't know what he was up to."

"Can you think of anyone we should be talking to? Any friends that could help in trying to catch who did this?"

Baron gave us the names of three guys Tinder ran around with while she was with him, and we left.

On the way to the car, I said, "Well, doesn't seem Chapman and Tinder knew each other."

"Maybe, but it's two years since they lived together."

Two of the names Baron gave us were a total waste of time. It's not like we expected them to talk like women in a hair salon, but the thugs were guarded, afraid they'd reveal something about their own criminal behavior.

We figured we'd have an easier time with the last guy, Joey Horchow, as he was sitting in the Stockade Road Jail in Immokalee. Boy, it sure seemed like everything was in or off Immokalee. We'd stop and have a chat with Horchow before going over to his dead buddy's apartment.

The Stockade Jail was a three-story, white cement building, encircled with ten-foot-high fencing, topped with razor wire. I'd been here so many times we didn't have to show our credentials to get through the gate.

Horchow was wearing a bored look and an orange jumpsuit. Comparing the mental image of his mug shot, something about him looked different. He'd been inside for just over three months as he awaited trial on a string of burglaries.

"This is Detective Vargas, and I'm Detective Luca. We're from homicide."

Horchow stiffened. "Homicide? I ain't got nothing to do with no murders."

"We're here to ask you about your buddy Brett Tinder."

"Oh. What about him?"

"He was murdered. Shot in the chest and dumped into the bay by Wiggins Pass."

"I heard."

"How'd you hear that?"

"Come on, man, you don't know nothing about jails? Anything on the outside gets in, just like water finds its way."

Water? Was that a signal?

"Hey, you got a smoke?"

"Smoking is not allowed."

"I'll take one back with me if you got one."

"What can you tell us about Tinder?"

"Why should I tell you anything?"

Vargas said, "Mr. Horchow, it's likely you'll be convicted and receive a sentence of ten to fourteen years—"

"If he's lucky."

She said, "Either way, you'll be going away for a long time. If you cooperate with us, we'll tell the prosecutor how helpful you've been. I can't promise anything more than that, but you're going to need all the help you can get if you expect to see daylight before your fiftieth birthday."

"What kinda stuff you want?"

I said, "Anything you know that could help our investigation into who killed him."

Vargas said, "You mentioned that information from outside seeps in here. What did you hear about his murder?"

"Not much, just that he was shot and was floating in the Cocohatchee."

"Who did it?"

He shook his head. "I donno. If I did, I'd be trading it to get outta here."

"Who had reason to do away with him? Anybody he had a beef with?"

"Brett was like two different people, you know. One day he would be going along, and next day, he was like, no way I'm doing that."

"Look, Joey, I like a riddle as much as the next guy, but what do you mean by that?"

"I gotta be careful. I say something and you gonna use it against me."

I said, "Unless you're talking about a homicide, nothing you say is going anywhere. Don't worry."

Vargas added, "And if it is a homicide, and you have information about it, we're prepared to negotiate an offer for the information."

"Man, I wish I had it, but Tinder was a thief, a fucking good one, but nothing more."

"So, what were you saying before about him being a chameleon?"

"Most of the jobs we worked, we did as teams. It makes it a lot safer."

Yeah, so safe you're sitting here looking at ten-plus years in the slammer. "Go on."

"What would piss guys off was we'd plan a job, and Brett would be all in one day, and then just before we'd do it, he'd pull out. He did it more than once, and it made guys mad, real mad."

"Mad enough to kill him?"

He shrugged.

"Anybody come to mind?"

"I donno."

"Come on, Joey."

"You really gonna talk with the judge and all?"

Vargas said, "Absolutely. We help each other here, and we both win."

"You sure?"

I said, "You have our word, Joey. Now, tell us, who do you think had it in for Tinder."

"Chenko. He never liked Brett, always bad-mouthed him. They had a big-assed fight one night, and Chenko pulled a knife on him. I swear, he would've sliced him to pieces if we didn't stop it."

"Where was this fight?"

"At the body shop we hung out at on Taylor."

"Where does this Chenko live, and does he have a first name?"

"Alex. He's out of Leigh Acres."

"Any idea why Tinder would be flip-flopping all the time?"

"Brett was a good guy, deep down. He liked kids—"

"And to beat his girlfriends up."

"He felt bad, really bad about it, but he had anger issues. He tried to control himself, even started going to church."

"Guess it didn't work."

"I donno. Since he was going to church, he didn't explode so much."

"How long did you know Joey Chapman?"

"Who?"

I offered a picture to him. "Joey Chapman."

He shook his head. "No idea who this is."

"Was Tinder gay?"

"You mean like a homo?"

"Yes."

"Nah, he was straight, man."

"You sure?"

"Uh-huh."

Vargas said, "Maybe your buddy was conflicted and had anger because he was confused about who he was. Does that make sense to you?"

"So, you saying he flipped out and beat his women because he was a queer?"

I said, "There are numerous examples of men who portray themselves as heterosexual but are really gay. It takes a toll, and they sometimes get violent, many times with women."

6

———

LIGHTS FLASHING, I SLOWED TO A CRAWL AS AN OFFICER moved cones to the side. Turning off Route 41, I drove on the wrong side of Immokalee Road. Traffic was blocked from Airport Polling to 41, and it was weird—there wasn't a car on the westbound side. Rubberneckers on the eastbound side had created a bumper-to-bumper jam trying to see what the police activity was about.

"You know, Vargas, if people were so curious about the rest of their lives, it'd be a better world."

We pulled up to the Palm River intersection, joining three patrol cars.

"Is that Bailey? I hope not."

"Yup."

"Last scene I worked with him on Keewaydin, he was trampling all over the damn place. I'm surprised he's not taking a swim down there."

"Oh, Frank, you always exaggerate."

"Hey, I'm not exaggerating when I tell you that you look good. Am I?"

Her smile brightened the mood for a moment.

We approached the drainage canal that ran alongside Immokalee. A couple of patrolmen, including Bailey, were gathered on the Palm River bridge intersection with their arms on the railing. Bailey saw us and said, "If it ain't George Clooney himself."

I considered tossing him over, but said, "What do we got?"

Bailey pointed toward the water. "Heckuva place to take a swim."

Leaning over the railing, there was a body pinned against a stanchion. Another floater. Based on the clothing and hair it looked male, but you never knew these days. I looked straight up the canal toward Airport Polling. Nothing stood out.

I said to Vargas, "This guy could've floated down from Collier Boulevard."

"We gotta check to see if all the locks were open."

"I'm betting, with not much rain, they were. I can't even remember the last time I saw them closed."

When I first came to this area I spent time familiarizing myself with a network of canals, basins, and ditches. The systems were used to control flooding and storm water runoffs, keeping water quality high while preserving the wetlands. It was effective, but what interested me were the possible ways criminals might use the system. This was the second body we'd found in the time I'd been here, and I was laying odds this guy had been killed as well.

I looked down at the body again. It was the third floater in less than a month. The current bobbed the corpse, and I said, "Tell Bailey to call Aquatics and have the locks shut. I don't want this guy floating into the Gulf."

Vargas said, "I think this canal feeds into the Cocohatchee."

I pointed at the dark clouds gathering in the east. "Whatever. It starts raining somewhere out east, feeding the canal, and our body will be in for a ride. And get him to have District One send a boat down here to help fish him out."

As Vargas instructed Bailey, I headed across the bridge and toward the bank. The canal sides were steep. Grabbing a large valve, I eased a couple of feet down the slope. There were no signs of a gunshot or a stabbing. Did this guy fall in? Was he drunk?

There was a legion of men, mostly younger, who fished in these canals. The idea grossed me out. The canal waters were pretty clean, but why the hell would you fish here with the Gulf of Mexico staring you in the face?

Vargas walked over. "What do you think?"

I shook my head. "Not sure. This guy could've been fishing and slipped, hit his head. Or was blitzed and—who knows?"

"It feels like these are connected, Frank."

"How so?"

"Water. The bodies are found in water."

I snickered. "First off, this is Southwest Florida, my dear. If you noticed, we've got ourselves a bit of water around here."

She shook her head. "Sometimes you're a real know-it-all, you know that?"

Oops. "Just kidding, Mary Ann. The Chapman guy was in a drainage gully, with no standing water."

"I was there. Remember?"

Keeping my wise mouth shut wasn't easy. I didn't want to piss her off. "I know. I'm just saying—"

"Well, next time think about how you say it."

I felt myself nodding as Vargas stormed off. Maybe this dating a partner thing wasn't such a good idea.

***

AFTER STICKING a pole in the water to measure the depth, two officers in chest-high waders shimmied down the bank, into the water. An aluminum, ladder-like sled was lowered off the bridge. The officers submerged the device, securing the body on it. They gave a thumbs-up, and the body rose, albeit not from the dead.

I helped two other officers hoist the contraption over the railing. Though soaked, I estimated its weight at a hundred and seventy pounds as we set it down on the pavement. The body was clad in skin-tight jeans and a green golf shirt.

As they untied the straps, I pulled on gloves, asking, "Can you turn him over?" As an officer knelt and grabbed his legs, I dipped into the corpse's back pocket and handed a soaked wallet to Vargas.

Before he was fully on his back, I could see blood stains on the front of his shirt. Two bullet holes were the source. I looked up at Vargas, expecting her to be smiling. She wasn't, and that's the thing about her; she was a much better person than I was.

The victim was Dick Cornwall, a thirty-seven-year-old who lived off Davis Boulevard. His face was marginally bloated, but, excepting the two bullet wounds, there were no visible injuries. Cornwall had tattoos on both forearms and had kept whatever hair he had left short. Men seemed to be going balder earlier and earlier. Was it something evolutionary?

"Mary Ann, your hands are smaller, check the front pockets."

Vargas squeezed her hand into the left pocket and came up with a pair of keys and three dimes. The right pocket held a pocket knife shaped like a fish.

She handed the knife to me. "This guy could've been fishing."

Opening the blade, I examined the fish-shaped implement. The side opposite the blade was shaped in a fish tail and was designed to open bottles. I said, "Maybe, or he carried it to open bottles of beer."

"You want me to have a search of the banks along the canal to see if any fishing gear is lying around?"

It was an idea I should have thought of as soon as I'd arrived on the scene. "Sure. Have them look all the way up to Collier Boulevard but call it in from the car. I wanna get back and find out who this guy was."

7

———

THERE WAS NO DOUBT I WAS GLAD TO SEE FRANK MORGAN go, but with a new sheriff, I'd have to prove myself to a fresh boss again. It was the third time in three years I'd have to build a relationship, and it was tiring and distracting.

Don Chester seemed like a decent guy and a law enforcement pro, but being new to the position and having what looked like a serial killer on the loose was enough to turn a puppy into a pit bull.

Without Vargas as a buffer, I was shown into the sheriff's office. Chester pushed back from his desk and stood. I liked the respect, but gone with the cowboy boots was the informality that made Morgan tolerable.

Chester buttoned his suit jacket, and hand extended, came around his desk.

"Detective Luca. It's good to see you again."

"Thank you, sir."

Chester had a law degree but was groomed like a Madison Avenue ad man and said, "Have a seat."

Circling back to his desk, he picked up a copy of the *Naples Daily News*. "Have you seen this?"

Shaking my head, I took the paper. The headline screamed, "Aquatic Assassin Strikes Again."

"Aquatic Assassin? They're branding to sell papers?"

"This hits the heart of our economy. We must find this nut, fast."

"We're working on it, sir, now that we believe it's the same killer."

"If you're unable to solve this quickly, I'm going to have to request assistance from the FBI."

I didn't have a problem with the G-men, but I needed more time. Besides, the FBI had quite a few swings and misses in the last year. "I don't believe that will be necessary, sir. We're confident we'll apprehend the person or persons responsible for these murders."

"I'm afraid we don't have much time, Detective Luca. The pressure to find this killer is building."

* * *

STARVING, I chewed on a bagel from the cafeteria and began reading emails. As I read one from forensics, I tossed the bagel in the trash and looked at the ceiling.

Even though I knew it, the confirmation was unsettling. This was the biggest case of my career, and I wasn't at my best. Three dead, and we were nowhere close to figuring out who the hell was responsible. This case was a make or break for me.

Demarcation points were coming at me like a driving rain. I'd gotten divorced, lost my former partner, moved down to Naples, gotten cancer, and was falling for my partner.

I was on fresh territory, both on the job and with what was happening with Mary Ann. This relationship thing could get complicated. As the senior homicide detective, I was her boss. Could I turn things off and on? I had to. Lives were at stake. Mary Ann would understand; she always got things before I did.

Reading the report again, there was no doubt the bullets that killed Chapman, Tinder, and Cornwall came from the same gun. We had a serial killer on our hands. I got up and paced, trying to think of any contacts I had up north, when my partner/girlfriend came in.

"What's the matter, Frank?"

"Ballistics report came back on Cornwall. Same gun as Chapman and Tinder."

"Okay, but we knew that."

"I know, but I guess it's the reality of it." I lowered my voice. "This is a big case, Mary Ann."

She put her hands on her hips. "You think I don't realize that?"

"No, no. It's just that, we've got to work hard and—"

She sighed. "What's up, Frank?"

Why couldn't she just read my mind entirely? "I'm just, you know, concerned about us. You know, we're doing good together. But I'm the lead here, and I don't want you, I mean, I can say stupid things on the job, and I don't want it to affect our relationship."

"So, that's it? You're worried about us?"

I nodded.

"That's thoughtful of you, Frank. No worries, okay?"

"Are you sure?"

She smiled. "Absolutely."

"That's great."

"And detective, just so you know, you don't say stupid things only when you're on the job."

VARGAS WAS outside the courthouse in a black SUV. I skipped down the stairs. Pulling the door open, I was hit with the smell of stale smoke.

"Geez, it smells like a damn ashtray."

"I know, you'll get used to it."

"I bet it was O'Reilly. He's a frigging chimney."

"Probably. You know that guy Horchow gave us, Alex Chenko? You're never going to believe where he is."

"Behind bars."

"Yep. He couldn't have done it—he was arrested earlier, the day before Tinder washed up."

"Just great. We got nothing, then."

"What about the homosexual angle, Frank?"

"We need more—a lot more than we have."

"Chapman was gay, and though we don't have proof, Tinder could've been. Maybe he swung from both sides of the plate."

"If the first killing wasn't Chapman, would we even be looking for an orientation angle?"

"I'd hope so, but you're right, we probably wouldn't."

"I'm not saying it isn't relevant, but for now let's park it."

8

———

Less than a week later, I was back in the sheriff's office. Chester was wearing a red tie and a worried look. He rose. I stuck out my hand, but he sat right back down, saying, "I just had a conversation with the governor. He's receiving flak from the hospitality industry. People are beginning to get worried. Bookings are trending downward."

"I understand, sir, but there's no connection. No tourists have been harmed or targeted. You ask me, I think this guy might be settling old scores."

"You have a particular theory?"

"We're developing several angles at this stage."

"The governor suggested we ask the FBI for assistance, have one of their profilers help steer us in the right direction."

"With all due respect, sir, I believe it's premature. I've taken several courses on profiling, two of them at the Hoover Building in DC. I just don't see the value at this point."

"I don't know about that, Detective Luca."

"It'd be a distraction, sir."

"I'm going to give this further consideration."

"I understand, sir."

The sheriff straightened his tie. "Please tell me what you have and the direction you are pursuing."

"We're exploring a couple of theories. There's been no evidence of raging violence, gunshot wounds excepted, so we're certain the killing is premeditated. Given the criminal backgrounds of the victims, it's possible these are revenge killings. The killer, or killers, may have been a victim of a crime perpetrated by the people he's killed."

"You believe he's finished killing?"

"It's a possibility, sir. If he's settled his scores, assuming that's what this is, he may be done."

"Is that what we're hoping? That whoever did this is finished?"

"I didn't mean to imply that was our main avenue of pursuit."

"What else do you have?"

"Well, we've recently learned that Chapman, the first victim, was homosexual. It could be that the killer had a relationship with him."

Chester tilted his head. "Or Chapman made unwelcome advances."

"That's possible, sir. Or it could be unrelated to a relationship and be a hate crime."

"But are any of the other two victims gay?"

"Not openly, but we're working backgrounds on each of them to see if they were."

"It's an angle to pursue, but you must be careful. We're going to need something tangible—and quick."

I SLAMMED THE DOOR. "Two days ago Chester said he'd give me time, and then he goes and gets the FBI involved."

Vargas said, "I thought you said he was giving it consideration."

"Whatever. It's bullshit. These guys come down from Washington like their shit don't stink. You should've seen this Haines guy, sitting there so smug. The twerp even dyes his hair."

"Take it easy, Frank. We can use the help."

"I don't like it. He wants to give us a profile, fine. But no more than that."

"It could help. You know, the first profiling ever was done on the Ted Bundy case, and it helped."

"Come on, Vargas, I took classes myself. Besides, Bundy was caught in a traffic stop. Look, it can help, but the next thing you know the Feds are crawling all over here, and we're on the outside. It's bullshit, I'm telling—"

There was a knock on the door before it swung open.

"Is this a good time, Detective?"

It was Tom Haines, the FBI agent.

"Sure, sure. Come on in. This is my partner, Detective Mary Ann Vargas."

Haines's eyes paused a little too long on Mary Ann. I said, "Have a seat. You want a coffee?"

"Nah, I'm trying like hell to cut back. Had four cups already."

I was dying for a cup but wasn't gonna leave him alone with Mary Ann. "I hear you. Okay, then, let's get right to it."

"Are you familiar with the process?"

Vargas said, "A little."

"Like I told you, I've taken courses on profiling."

With his whitened teeth, Haines smiled at Mary Ann and said, "Good. This is going to be substantially more in-depth, and we've developed a couple new practices that have proved useful."

This guy was a know-it-all, and Mary Ann was leaning forward like a six-year-old at a magic show.

"Tell me about the victims and crime scenes."

I CLOSED the door behind Haines and turned to Vargas. "Thank God for the FBI. Can you imagine, the killer is a white male who's intelligent? How the hell would we have figured that out?"

"He just got here, Frank. We've got to give him a chance. We need the help."

"He and Chester are wasting our time. We both agreed it was likely a male who was smart enough or careful enough not to leave evidence. I don't need a damn Washington profiler. What I need is a connection between the victims, or else we're just looking for a nutjob who randomly chooses his victims."

"Like you always say, Frank, we do the work, and the clues will start piling up."

"Yeah, but this time we've got Haines and Chester breathing down our necks."

"You're getting a little paranoid, Frank."

"Really?"

"Yes. Really. Haines seems like a nice guy. It's not his fault he's here. And besides, he has a lot of experience with serial killers."

"So, now you're defending him?"

Mary Ann shook her head and got up. "I never thought I'd say it, but I'm sure glad I'm due in court in an hour."

I pushed it too far, again. "I'll see you later, okay?"

On her way out the door she said, "I guess so."

I guess so? Weren't we going on a date tonight?

9

———

WE WALKED THROUGH A PACKED, GLASS-ENCLOSED ROOM AT HB's On the Gulf and out onto the patio. A drier than usual breeze, infused with the smell of heated sand, swept away most of the tension between us.

The beach was behind a low wall and still had a few hangers-on waiting for the sunset. I popped on my sunglasses as we were shown to a table on the cusp of the sand. A bartender friend, who worked the beach bar, had come through again. It seemed unlikely, but there was a bond between cops and bartenders—maybe it was they were good listeners—who oftentimes offered free drinks. Or maybe they appreciated how often we were called in to make the peace when fights broke out.

"This is nice, Frank."

Score one for Luca. "Only the best for you, Mary Ann."

"It's funny, I've never been here, and it's one of the few places you can eat on the water."

"It's kinda weird, though. You go through this giant lobby before you get outside, and it's also a beach club, with people in their bathing suits. I like it better in the winter, when it gets darker earlier—it's got a different vibe."

"But you can't see the water."

"You can hear it."

A waiter came by, and remembering they had reasonable offerings, I asked for the wine list.

"Wine again?"

"I'm starting to get into it. You know that Barnet guy; he was a badass, but he gave me a couple of ideas."

I looked through the list. Nothing looked familiar. I looked at the right-hand column and found a Malbec for forty-two dollars.

The server brought it out immediately. He screwed off the top, dialing down the romance a notch, and poured a splash into my glass.

It felt like the entire restaurant was looking at me. Remembering Barnet at his store, I stuck my nose into the glass and inhaled. I gave him a thumbs-up, and the waiter filled our glasses.

We clinked glasses. "Salute."

I guzzled a glass and poured another, trying to recall the way Barnett described a wine. The Malbec tasted dark, maybe deeper than blueberries?

"You seem a little uptight, Frank."

She could read me like a book. I liked that, but if the two of us went anywhere, I'd never get away with anything.

"I'm okay. Just takes me a little time to go from work to play."

"You didn't have any problem at Blue Martini's happy hour."

She didn't know that I'd had a glass of wine before she got there yesterday.

"You think anybody knows about us?"

Vargas shrugged. "I don't know. I never said anything."

As a waiter delivered a plate of giant shrimp to the next table, I said, "Me either. It's nobody's business anyway."

She raised a glass. "Amen."

"Do you think it's against the department's rules?"

She leaned over. "I called HR—"

"What?"

"Take it easy. It's a general line for applicants. They said spouses can both work for the department, but they have to be on different shifts."

"We're screwed, then."

"We getting married?"

The glass slipped out of my hand, spilling wine all over the tablecloth. Rushing over, a busboy laid a napkin over the purple stain.

Mary Ann put her hand on mine. "Relax, Frank. We'll figure this all out. Take a look at that sky. It's so pretty."

The sky was taking on a reddish orange hue as the sun fell into the Gulf.

"You know, up in Jersey, I never paid attention to the sky or sunsets." I wasn't sure if it was the cancer or the geography that focused things. "But down here you can't avoid it."

"It's beautiful."

I heard myself say, "Just like you."

Mary Ann grabbed my face between her hands and planted a kiss on my lips. Then she picked up the menu. "What are you having?"

"Hey, put that menu down and finish what you started. Otherwise, I have to haul you in for domestic abuse."

SUIT JACKET SLUNG over my shoulder, I was leaving to testify in an assault case when my email chimed. Leaning over, I saw the sender was the Sheriff. Plopping into my chair, I opened the email as Vargas came in.

"What are you still doing here?"

"Just reading an email from the Sheriff. He wants a progress update on the serial killer."

"We don't really have much."

I shook my head instead of saying thanks for reminding me.

Vargas said, "We've got to tell him something."

"Didn't think I'd ever say this, but I'm glad I'm due in court. You have to do it."

"No problem."

"Do me a favor. Since he seems to like you better than me, when he starts in with the FBI stuff, try to buy a little time for us."

"Magician, I'm not."

"I gotta run."

I TEND to exaggerate the negative impact lawyers have on society, but today it was justified. My slotted time to testify was one p.m. It was an estimate, just like going to an arrogant doctor's appointment who couldn't care less about your time. But it was four p.m. when I put my hand on the Bible, making me late for another look at a place to live.

Airport Polling was packed, and I was so worked up that I missed the turnoff for Goodlette while talking to Vargas. Route 41 was wall-to-wall cars approaching Golden Gate. I called the agent, but she couldn't change the time because she had to pick up her kid from baseball practice.

It had been a year since I'd been cited for using my siren and lights in a nonemergency situation. I checked my mirrors and flipped both switches. As cars moved to the right, I snaked my way into the Golden Gate intersection, made a right, and headed for Goodlette.

Located in a prime area, Autumn Woods was a quiet community of full-timers. The house I was seeing was too big for me, but I agreed to consider it because of the location and my shortening time line.

I made my way to Old Banyan Way, realizing most of the houses were one-level places. How come the only one for sale was a two-story house?

As I pulled up, the door on a white Audi SUV opened, and the agent stepped out. The perky forty-year-old looked twice at her watch before meeting me in the driveway.

She handed me the listing, opened the door, and told me she had to make a call. The place was empty, so there was a lot of wiggle room in the price. I had my own way of going through a house, and it always started with the dining room.

Problem was, it had a formal living room opposite the dining room. I didn't even need a dining room, no less a living room. It was a shame. The house had good natural light and clean lines. I tried to think of some way to use the space as I headed to the kitchen.

The cabinets were off-white and wood, capped with cream-colored granite. It was nice, opening to a large family room. I wished the ceilings were higher, but this place had a second story.

The master was too big by half, and a second bedroom and large study rounded out the first floor. As soon as I reached the top of the stairs and saw a second family room, I turned around and headed down. The place was too big and too expensive for me.

I told the agent that I liked the place, which was true, and that I would consider making an offer, which wasn't. On the ride home, I pondered the importance of tomorrow morning's outing.

10

——————

Thankful for the cool air, I stepped out of a humid August morning and into the foyer, where the music got louder. A near capacity crowd was visible through a pair of glass doors leading to the main part of The Spirit of Fellowship Church. Slipping inside, the congregation swayed to what seemed to be Christian rock music. My foot involuntarily began tapping as I surveyed the crowd. Were there any clues to who might be the next victim?

Scanning right, there had to be a least forty rows making up the Epistle side. I realized the floor plan resembled a cross. Dead center, in front of the alter, at the top of the cross, a man, arms raised, encouraged the singing. He was wearing a dark suit and a red tie. I squinted. Was that Minister Gabriel Booth? Taking a step closer confirmed it. The band segued into a song that began with repeated phrases of Our Savior. It was redundant as all hell, but I found myself singing it softly.

The music slowed and faded. It was just past eleven. The service must be over, as it kicked off at ten. Minister Booth grabbed the microphone, and the parishioners took seats.

Heading left, I slipped into a pew on the Gospel side as the keyboardist began melodically tinkling the keys.

"Brothers and sisters, we've celebrated the promise of eternal life, but in order to redeem the promise our Savior made, we must live as children of God. We must earn our way to salvation. There are no free passes in this life. We shouldn't shy from speaking the Gospel and living our lives as God has told us." Booth raised the Bible. "God has made it easy for us; he left us the instructions right here. All we have to do is follow them. Who could ask for more?" The congregation cheered.

Really? I get the New Testament message, but the rest of the Bible? It didn't speak to me. In fact, it was tough, if not impossible, to read. How could you get a message out of that? I tried but couldn't line up with reading ten pages of gobbledygook to find a sentence that was supposed to be mean something.

Booth gently set the Bible on the altar and stepped up into a pulpit. He surveyed the audience before speaking,

"God is testing us. Every day, in every way. He gives us an unfathomable number of opportunities to demonstrate we hear his instruction. Earlier today, we heard from Ephesians 4:32, 'And Be kind to one another, tenderhearted, forgiving one other, even as God in Christ forgave you.' God is calling us to love one another. Will we listen?"

Booth put his hands on the pulpit. "Are we listening? I think not. We are sliding into incivility. If we do not right our ways, we will spend eternity in the blazes of hell. I beseech you to heed his message; change your ways. God is a loving God, but we will suffer his wrath if we do not repent and change."

A chorus of amens broke out.

As the minister continued preaching, warning and scolding for a solid fifteen minutes, I studied his followers. It was tough to get a read. Most were dressed in clothes that would have barred entry when I was a teenager. Craning my neck, it hit me there were more men than women in attendance. That seemed unusual, as it was women who filled all the churches I'd ever been in.

Remembering St. Mary's Church, where I went to mass as a child, brought a wave of guilt. I'd drifted, like most adults, away from religion. Comforting myself with self-talk that I was a good person and God knew that, a pair of monitors came to life displaying rolling Bible passages.

Minister Booth stepped down from the pulpit. He stood at the cross's intersection and shouted, "Whether we fail or pass is up to us. Will you enter the gates of heaven or burn in hell?"

The congregation shot out of their seats and applauded as the band broke into a catchy tune about walking with Jesus. They did the music right there. It was so different from what I was used to. The other thing different was no one rushed for the exits when the service ended. At St. Mary's, the trickle of people leaving right after Communion would be joined by most before the final hymn even began. Here people were in no rush and hung around talking.

There were a set of tables filled with literature outside the foyer where Booth and a woman, I suspected was his wife, chatted with parishioners as they left. Passing over leaflets titled, *The Purpose of Stripping the Adulteress in Hosea, All Together for Asylum Justice*, and *Biblical Responses to Homosexuality*. I picked up *The Community is Your Family*. I read it, and when I set it back down, there were still people talking with Booth. Wishing this place was more like St.

Mary's, I headed for the bathroom, hoping the ten minutes it would take me to pee would be enough to clear the place.

My timing was perfect; Booth was shaking the hands of the last person. I went up to the minister.

"Minister Booth, I'm Detective Luca. I'd like to come by tomorrow for a quick chat."

11

———

Minister Booth was in his office with a parishioner when his secretary told him I was waiting. Five minutes later the minister came out, his hand on an older woman's shoulder. He told her not to worry, that he'd get back to her as she left.

"I'm sorry to have kept you waiting, Detective. But that poor woman, she came in unexpectedly, and it's my duty to help when asked."

We shook hands. "No problem. Good to see you."

"Come, sit. Can I get you anything? Coffee? Water?"

I didn't want to start off saying I had to watch my fluids intake.

"Thanks. I'm fine."

"I'm sure you're busy, but would you mind if I grabbed a cup of coffee?"

"Go right ahead."

"Sure you wouldn't like one?"

"No thanks."

My initial read was that Gabriel Booth was about as unguarded a person as I'd ever met. It could be an act. I cautioned myself not to be misled by his position as a minister and scanned the room. A red-and-blue sign proclaiming, The Bible - God's Instruction Manual for Life, dominated the room.

The furniture was older and modest. Booth had a simple desk with a picture of his blond wife next to a worn Bible. There were two diplomas hanging on a wall. One from Trinity Evangelical Divinity School, and the other from Northern Seminary. Below the pigskins, a burning candle, with a vanilla scent, was centered on a drawer-less wooden table.

Coffee cup in hand and apologies flowing, Booth closed the door to his office and sat down.

"I'm still uncertain why you wanted to see me."

I exhaled. "I'm sure you're aware of the, so-called, Aquatic Assassin. Well, two of his victims apparently came to your church."

Booth set his cup down as the color drained out of his face. "I heard that one of our newer members, Brett Tinder, I believe his name was, had been murdered."

"Yes, that's him. There's a second man, Dick Cornwall, who we believe was murdered by the same killer and who we believe attended your church."

Booth scrunched his face. "Cornwall? I don't believe I've met him." He stood. "Hold on, let me have Miriam check the records."

Returning, Booth said, "Dick Cornwall was a new member. He formally registered just a month ago. I'm not sure why I can't recall him. I usually meet the new members."

That was an interesting admission. I wasn't sure there was something behind that, and asked, "Did you have a funeral service for him?"

"No. I would have presided over it, and though my memory is not what it once was, I'd remember that."

"Can I have some background on your church? It might provide a clue to the murders."

Booth tucked his chin in. "You think there's a connection between these murders and my church?"

"We're looking at every possible angle, and the fact that two of your members, both with criminal backgrounds, were targeted, is tough to ignore."

Booth straightened his shoulders. "Detective, many of our members have lived lives that led them astray. But that doesn't mean we should give up on them. Everyone can be redeemed. everyone can change, be born again into a new life, one where God is at the center."

I wanted to cite recidivism rates that'd show the minister that change, if it happened, was an uphill climb.

"It's my understanding that—"

The door opened and a large, well-proportioned woman, whose blond hair was piled on the top of her head, entered gingerly. She was wearing a drab, loose-fitting dress that couldn't hide a certain sexiness.

"Hi, Hannah. Detective, this is my wife, Hannah."

I got up to shake her hand, but she didn't offer one. A calculation was taking place behind her eyes, and it wasn't until she forced a smile that I realized her blue eyes were stunning.

The Minister asked her, "How's your back?"

"The same. What's going on?"

"Detective Luca is investigating the serial killer. It seems the last victim was also a member, a poor soul named Dick Cornwall."

She showed zero emotion and didn't move closer to her husband, which I found odd. Usually a spouse moves nearer in a show of support. I didn't think Booth was involved, but it would be nice to see.

I asked, "Did you know Brett Tinder and Dick Cornwall, Mrs. Booth?"

"Yes."

"And how did you know them?"

"Through the church."

Did she have legal training? I didn't like this woman and couldn't imagine having dinner with her every night like the minister did. He really was a man of God.

With limited time, I turned my attention back to Gabriel Booth. "I wanted to ask about the church's reputation. I understand you're known to do a lot of work with drug addicts and former inmates."

Miss Congeniality said, "'Peter asked, Lord, how many times will my brother sin against me and I forgive him? As many as seven times?' Jesus answered, 'I do not say seven times but seventy times seven.'"

The minister said, "As Hannah quotes Matthew 18:21, God demands that we forgive those who go astray, asking us to extend ourselves to them, help them overcome Satan."

I felt myself nodding. "I understand, but on a practical level, what do you do at the church?"

"First and foremost is to welcome all. We don't care about what you did in the past. We want to help you live your life the way God intended."

"Do you operate specific programs to address, say, the particular needs of recovering addicts?"

"We don't profess to have the medical or psychological expertise that comes from outside sources, but we know those programs are more likely to succeed when supplemented by the love and support we freely offer. What we have is a buddy system mirrored on the one at Alcoholics Anonymous. Oftentimes, when one loses their way, their families and friends abandon them. We try to fill that void with someone who has overcome similar struggles. Someone who understands their particular situation."

A solid plan, and I was rooting for this guy to change the world, but in the meantime, my job was safe. I asked, "Can you check on whether Joseph Chapman was a member here?"

"Chapman? No, I don't think so. Hannah, do you know him?"

"No."

Her reply came a little too quickly. Did she have a reason, maybe in her past, to distrust the police? It had to be, because if she was somehow mixed up in this, she was doing a piss-poor job of hiding it.

Gabriel rose. "I'll go ask Miriam if she knows anything."

Hannah said, "Don't. She left for lunch."

Who needed air-conditioning when this woman was around?

"Oh, well, when she gets back then, we'll check and let you know." He picked up a pen.

When the minister finished writing Chapman's name, I asked, "Would either of you know the sexual orientations of Brett Tinder and Dick Cornwall?"

Gabriel shifted in his chair. "I couldn't answer definitively, but I believe Brett was heterosexual."

"How about you, Mrs. Booth?"

"How would I know?"

I wanted to say, perhaps one of them made a pass at you, but considering the threat of frostbite, that was unreasonable.

"So, you have no knowledge, then?"

"I only knew Brett. As Minister Booth said, he appeared to like women."

She addresses her husband as Minister Booth?

"Can you think of anyone, a member of the church or not, that had an argument or conflict of some kind with Brett Tinder?"

"We have a special community here, Detective, and don't tolerate mean-spirited behavior. It would destroy the supportive, brotherly environment we foster at The Spirit of Fellowship Church. There's no one that comes to my mind. How about you, Hannah?"

The minister's wife shook her head.

12

———————

The hotline we'd established to snare leads hadn't given us anything other than the normal—people who thought their neighbor was strange or who were afraid. We needed more.

I never liked getting in front of a camera, but pleas for information always generated higher response rates when the rank and file made them. It was more proof of the distrust Americans have with smooth-talking people with power.

Tips from the public were a vital source of leads, despite having to check into scores of time wasters. To be sure we covered as large a demographic as possible, Vargas and I were both going to make an appeal for help.

Mary Ann told me to wear a sport jacket but no tie, and she wore a navy-colored pantsuit that was nowhere near my favorite. We were sweltering in a Publix parking lot when the word came we were going live. The video would be distributed to all television outlets and spliced into their coverage of the serial killer. It was miles easier than making the rounds with every network and local station.

The reporter asked, "Detective Luca, what would you like to say to the public?"

"These murders were brutal. We're asking for the public's help in solving the killings." I looked straight into the camera. "If you have any information relating to the so-called Aquatic Assassin killings, we ask that you call our hotline at 855-888-9000. The person or persons responsible for these shootings are dangerous. Do not attempt to engage them. please call the police."

Vargas said, "We urge you to come forward quickly. Your information will be held strictly confidential. No matter the circumstances of how you've gained any knowledge, you can be assured it will remain anonymous if you choose. Please, we need your help before anyone else is harmed."

I said, "Any information you may have could be critical to apprehending the person or persons responsible for these murders. Please call our confidential, toll free hotline at 855-888-9000. This is a private number. Your call will not be traced. Thank you for helping to get this killer off the streets. As a token of appreciation, the county has offered a reward of one hundred thousand dollars for information leading to the arrest of the killer. Here's the number again, 855-888-9000. Thank you."

THE MORNING after the plea aired I was at my desk, sorting through emails when the phone rang. It was the officer running the hotline.

"Hey Frank, there's two calls we think should be run down. Both of them aren't concerned with confidentiality. In fact, the first guy seemed like he wanted to talk."

I grabbed a pen. "Feed me."

"The talker was this guy, Tony Kelp. He sounds older, lives in one of those buildings off Vanderbilt. He said he thought he heard a gunshot the night Tinder was found in the pass."

I jotted down Kelp's contact details. "Okay, what else?"

"Woman, Justine Francis, saw a car the night Chapman was shot."

I took down her address and said, "Anything else?"

"Wish I had more for you, Frank, but out of the seventy calls we got, these were the only ones worth chasing."

"Thanks. If anything else comes in, let me know. Chester is all over this, and I'd rather get them as they come in."

I hung up, called the two leads, and headed out to interview them.

JUSTINE FRANCIS LIVED in a condo off of Deerwood Lane in Lely Resort. I was surprised but glad there was no gate to get through. Maybe it was being in law enforcement that made me dislike the false sense of security the gates provided.

Justine was a big-framed woman who looked to be in her late sixties. I liked her instantly. Hair a silvery tone, Justine was one of those lucky ladies who didn't have to dye it, though she made up for it by pounding on the makeup. She spoke in a soft voice that didn't quite fit her size.

"It's really frightening to know the killer is still out there."

There was a hint of Febreze in the air. "We're working around the clock to apprehend those responsible. I don't believe you have anything to fear, ma'am."

"I hope not. Can I get you some coffee?"

"Only if it's made."

"I have one of those pod machines. Follow me to the kitchen. Cream or sugar?"

Cream? Who serves cream at home? "Just a tiny bit of milk if you have it."

She set a mug, emblazoned with the Naples Zoo logo, on the table and told me to take a seat. The coffee was almost pure white. Why couldn't anyone just put a little milk in? Especially when asked for it that way.

"Thank you, ma'am. I wanted to thank you for calling the hotline. We appreciate any help we get to keep our neighborhoods safe."

She smiled. "I hope I can help, Detective."

Pulling out my Moleskine, I asked, "Why don't you tell me what you saw the night of June twenty-fourth?"

"I was driving on Wilson Boulevard and saw this car on the other side of the street."

"What time was that?"

"About eight or a little after."

"What made the car stand out; why'd you notice it?"

"I donno, really. It was raining, and I'm pretty sure it was the only car I saw going home."

"Where were you coming from?"

A bit of blush came through all the makeup. "My boyfriend's. You see, my husband—we were married for thirty-seven years—he had a heart attack and passed away just over five years ago."

Five years? That seemed like more than enough time in my book. "Okay. Did you notice the color of the car?"

She shook her head. "It was dark. I donno, maybe black or a blue—maybe it was brown."

I lost hope we'd be able to identify the car. "Any idea on the type of car? You know, was it a four-door?"

She brightened. "Oh yes. It was a Honda, four doors."

What? "How can you be so sure?"

"My son Jimmy—he lives in Michigan—he has one just like it."

"Excellent."

It really wasn't excellent; there must be at least twenty thousand Hondas in Collier County.

"Did you happen to see how many people were in the car?"

She closed her eyes. "Hmm. I donno. I'm pretty sure there was somebody on the passenger side but wouldn't swear to it."

"Male driver?"

She nodded. "Yes, I'm pretty sure about that."

"Any idea on the age of the driver?"

"Kinda the same age as my son. Jimmy's gonna be thirty-seven in November."

"Did you happen to notice the license plate?"

"I can't say I did. Sorry."

"That's fine. Can you recall even seeing a front plate on the car?"

"I'm really sorry. I didn't think to look at the time. I didn't realize it would be important."

"That's fine. It's no problem. Let's go over this again."

We went over what she saw, and Francis kept to her story. I thanked her and left for the second caller, thinking of ways to track down a dark-colored Honda sedan.

It was my first time at Aqua, a high-rise development in Pelican Isle. It was in North Naples by Wiggins Pass. I'd seen a couple of ads for the condos, and boy, were they pricey. I didn't think you could get one for under two million.

Aqua was made up of three shapely buildings, nestled among a marina and had nice Gulf views. Tony Kelp lived in the northernmost building. Seeing its location was near the area where Tinder was found raised my hopes.

Kelp asked me to call him when I got through the gate. Parked in a visitor spot, I hopped out and dug my cell out, dialing as I walked to the water's edge. I called six times but kept getting his voice mail. I went to the front desk where the doorman said he thought he saw Mr. Kelp leave.

I hung around for another forty minutes, calling Kelp every fifteen minutes before leaving. Where the hell was this guy? Was something going on here?

13

———

NOTHING BURNED ME UP MORE THAN A HYPOCRITE. AND Shaun was among the worst offenders. Additionally, the son of wickedness looked similar to the lowlife who killed my mother. Listening to him lecturing others like he was some saint was painful. He had damn nerve telling people to get right with God. He was a perverted thug, abusing young girls and stealing anything that wasn't nailed down. The final straw was his dip into the collection box.

Shaun said, "You all right? You're quiet as all hell."

I nodded. "Just praying. Fell behind today. It's no excuse, but my day was extremely busy."

"Whatever."

"I know it's a bit late, but do you mind if we make a quick detour?"

Shaun said, "What's up?"

"Gideon asked me to do something for him and the church."

"That's cool by me."

He fiddled with the radio, settling on a station that had

annoying rap music playing. I turned onto Santa Barbara, and he said, "Where we going, all the way out here?"

"Gideon wanted us to explore the area out here. He wants to expand the church and was thinking of a satellite location."

Crossing over Radio Road, Shaun said, "That'd be something, huh? Two locations. Maybe he'd let me do more. Maybe even help run it."

This thieving idiot was delusional. "He tells me he likes you so, why not?"

We passed through the Davis Boulevard intersection, and he said, "It's dead out here. There's nothing—no buildings, no nothing."

"Guess that's why Gideon likes it. I'm sure it's much cheaper out here."

"That's got to be it."

I slowed down as a road wall protecting a community ended. There was nothing on either side of the road for at least two miles and no headlights in sight. Pulling onto the grass, I slowed to a crawl just shy of County Road.

Shaun said, "It's so damn dark out here, can't see nothing."

"What, are you scared?"

"Just a little spooky, that's all."

I stopped the car, reached under the seat and pulled out my gun.

"What do you got that for?"

I smiled and pointed it at Shaun.

"Come on, stop fucking around with that."

"Get out of the car. Slowly."

"What are you talking about? I ain't getting out."

Pressing the muzzle against his temple, I said, "You certainly are. Out!"

"Are you fucking crazy?"

"Now. Get out!"

Opening the door, Shaun's lips trembled. "You can't leave me out here. How am I gonna get home?"

"Don't worry about that. Now, back up."

"There's a fucking canal right here."

Sliding to the passenger seat, I opened the window, raising the gun up.

"Stop fucking around. Let's get out of here."

"Matthew 6:5 'And when you pray, do not be like the hypocrites, for they love to pray standing in the synagogues and on the street corners to be seen by others.'"

"What the fuck are you talking about?"

Squeezing the trigger, I fired two shots in rapid succession. They hit his chest, and Shaun toppled into the canal. I looked around—nothing. My back needed stretching, but I couldn't take a chance getting out of the car.

Pulling onto Santa Barbara, my hand fished for the shell casings. I smiled, The Lord's Sword had cast a smidgen of chaff aside.

As I made a right onto Rattlesnake Hammock Road, I felt a surge of pride in doing the Lord's work. Removing irredeemable sinners one by one wasn't going to make heaven on earth, but it was progress, and I was emboldened by Gideon's wisdom to be unconcerned about the temperature of the ocean, only the water around your ankles.

14

WHY WAS SANTA BARBARA BOULEVARD THREE LANES IN each direction? It didn't make sense, it was dead once you passed Davis. It didn't look like Naples to me. There must be a lot of developing coming out this way, as the infrastructure was in place already. If so, the politicians were thinking ahead for once. How about that?

Vargas pulled behind a caravan of parked police cars, and before the car was stopped, I popped the door open and the humidity flooded in. Hanging my head out, I took a deep breath, hoping to choke down the bile. I'd spit up the bagel I grabbed waiting for Vargas and hadn't been able to keep anything down since the news broke that another body had been found.

"We can't be doing this every two weeks. We've gotta catch this bastard, Vargas."

"We will—we always do."

She was too optimistic for me. I knew eventually whoever did it would get caught. But I was a helluva a lot less certain I'd be leading the case when it happened.

"Chester left me a message. He reach out to you?"

She nodded. "I called back and told Becky we'd report back after we were done here."

We limboed under the yellow tape and stepped on the grass. It was firm and dry, traces of dew excepted.

I said, "Hey, everyone! Pull back to the road. I don't want the scene trampled."

Vargas glanced my way, and I said, "It didn't rain last night, did it?"

"Not by me."

I looked up at a darkening sky. "Maybe forensics will be able to pick something up before it pours. That is, if these clowns didn't already contaminate things."

"You smell that?"

"Yeah, what is that?"

"I don't know, Frank. Maybe a fire."

"This time of the year, with all the rain?

"Maybe someone's burning their trash or something."

I looked around at the desolate area, certain there were a few yahoos out here who'd do that.

As the officers retreated, we checked to be sure no one disturbed the scene. Satisfied, Mary Ann and I stepped to the canal's edge. The bottom of the ten-foot-wide drainage canal was visible.

"We got a shot. At least the victim is not submerged in water this time."

Crouching at the same time was an interesting development in the relationship arena. We hung our heads over the edge. Lying on an angle, his upper back and head above the water, was another thirty-something white male.

"Looks like at least one gun shot, no?"

I said, "Tough to see, but looks like it."

Mary Ann stood and pointed. "There's a walkway."

We walked about fifty yards, crossing over a catwalk that topped a debris screen. The view from the other side was better but did nothing to clarify the situation. As we walked back over the narrow walkway, the coroner's van pulled up.

———

IT WAS SEVENTH GRADE AGAIN, and we were sitting in front of the principal. Chester had both of his palms on his desk and was drumming the fingers of his right hand. He stared at us like we were the damn bad guys.

Chester shifted in his chair, and a stream of sunlight blinded me. He said, "I want you to explain this. What theories do you have? What we are dealing with?"

Vargas moved to speak but I waved her off, shifting out of the sun, saying, "You're not going to like this, sir, but we don't know exactly what we have now."

The sheriff muttered, "Just great."

"The ballistics of the gun used to kill Shaun Parker doesn't match the other victims. They ran it multiple times, and it's not a match."

Vargas said, "This may be a copycat killing or simply that the killer used another gun."

I said, "The killer's MO was consistent, but the body wasn't completely in the water. Either it didn't go as planned, or it's not the same killer. What is interesting is, for the first time, we have forensic evidence to work with."

Chester said, "That could mean either the killer is getting careless, or it is, in fact, a copycat scenario."

"Exactly. We know all killers, no matter how careful, eventually make mistakes, get sloppy, or overconfident. We're hoping the hairs found on Parker will lead someplace."

"Hope is not enough, detectives. Do you have any idea how terrified the public is?"

"We understand, sir. But they really have nothing to fear."

Chester bolted upright. "Really?"

Vargas jumped in. "What Detective Luca is saying is that this killer seems to be targeting white males in their thirties."

"And what is his or her motivation? We don't have a shred of evidence to support that, making solving this case more difficult than it needs to be." He slammed a palm on the desk. "And you know who I blame for that? The two of you. Now, I want concrete progress, and I want it fast or you're off this case. Do I make myself clear?"

Instead of telling Chester to fuck himself, I nodded.

WE WERE SITTING at a table in Rosedale. It was empty and closing in twenty minutes. I don't think they would have let us in if they hadn't known me.

A pimply kid delivered our pizza, and I reached for a slice. Folding a slice, I blew on it and took a bite. It was hot as hell but good. Mary Ann was still cutting her piece up as I took another bite. Mouth full, I said, "I can't believe my career is hanging on two pieces of hair."

Mary Ann swallowed and put her fork down. "You're being a bit dramatic, Frank."

"You think so? I don't come up with something fast, Chester's gonna take me off the case."

Mary Ann sipped a cheap Chianti. "We'll come up with something."

"Where we gonna get something fast?"

"The sheriff directed forensics to drop what they were doing to concentrate on the Parker crime scene."

"They're not gonna get lucky, I can—"

"Someone's always saying: 'We keep our heads down, do the grunt work, interview away, and presto, our luck changes.'"

She didn't know it, but I hated it when she threw a saying of mine back at me. I took another piece of pizza.

"Easy for you to say. It ain't your career on the line."

"Geez, Frank. It's one case and a tough one. Stop feeling sorry for yourself and eat your damn pizza."

"Don't it bother you? I feel like I'm in quicksand."

"Look, I'm as frustrated as you are, but you gotta keep things in perspective, Frank. You can't define yourself by what goes on day to day."

"What the heck does that mean?"

"First off, your job is just your job, it's not who you are."

"But I like my job. It's a big part of me and who I am."

Mary Ann sighed. "Let me put it another way. When you do well, don't let it get to your head, and when you do poorly, don't let it get to your heart."

Nodding slowly, I had to admit it was a damn good saying, even if I didn't come up with it.

"Does that make sense, Frank?"

"Yeah, but I don't want to look like a fool in front of the entire force. If Chester relieves me of this case, it'd be embarrassing as all hell."

"Chester's got a job to do, and he's got to be seen as taking action. We can't control that."

"We damn well can. You see, that's where you're wrong, Mary Ann. If we make progress he's got to keep us on it."

"Who cares who solves this, as long as it's solved?"

I drained my wine glass and grabbed the last slice before I could say something stupid.

"So that's it, isn't it? Detective Frank Luca wants to be the hero. Give me a break."

"I—I—that's not true." Even though it was.

"Let's go. I'm tired."

15

THE FOLLOWING MORNING I WAS STUDYING A WALL OF pictures from the four crime scenes. Usually my internal voice would whisper something. But nothing this time—complete silence. The phone rang, and I tripped rushing to get it.

"Take it easy, Frank."

It was human resources reminding me to sign a document acknowledging receipt of the new employee handbook.

"Every day, more bureaucratic bullshit to deal with."

"You complaining again?"

"It just gets me, all this politically correct crap instead of focusing on the bad guys."

"You just woke up to the fact the lawyers are in charge?"

"It's a wonder we get anything done." The phone rang again.

After listening to the caller, I slammed the receiver down.

Vargas said, "Guess that wasn't good."

"No match on the hair or ballistics against the database. The gun's a 9mm, probably a Glock."

"It was a long shot."

"Now what?"

"Come on, Frank. All of a sudden you don't know what to do? Maybe Chester is right; we shouldn't be on this case."

"That's bullshit, and you know it! Clean up what you're doing. We're outta here in ten." I grabbed the Parker file to read while coaxing a pee out.

THE SIGN SAID SUNNY MEADOWS, but there wasn't a meadow in sight in the mobile home park on Radio Road. It was less than a mile from where Tinder had his apartment. Was there a connection?

Shaun Parker's brother lived in unit 62, a faded blue, single-wide trailer. The place was way past its mobile expiration date. The only way the heap would move was with a crane.

A warm drizzle began as I rapped on the door. A stocky guy, barefoot and in shorts, opened the door, holding a giant-sized soda from Burger King.

"Billy Parker?"

"Yeah, that's me. What do you want?"

I introduced ourselves, telling him we needed background information on his brother. Vargas followed with her condolences, and he moved aside to let us in.

Billy said he only had ten minutes, as he was getting ready to get to work. We went into what functioned as the kitchen. I'd seen platters bigger than this guy's kitchen table, but what caught my attention was what was on it.

The table was laden with wrappers from two burgers, three containers of fries, a milk shake, and a chocolate fudge sundae. I looked around for a note. This guy wasn't going to work; he was committing suicide.

Vargas asked, "Is there anyone you know who'd have any reason, no matter how deranged, to do this to Shaun?"

"Can't say I do. You know me and Shaun, we ain't so close. After Mom died, he started getting into all kinds of trouble, and I had no time for that bullshit. I mean, how many times you got to get thrown in jail to learn a lesson?"

She asked, "Who's older?"

"Me, by four years."

"Any other siblings."

"Nah, just the two of us, but like I say, we didn't keep in touch much."

I said, "When was the last time you saw him?"

He hesitated. "Probably Christmas."

"And you don't remember that?"

"Hey, man, look. Like I said, we weren't close."

The place was feeling claustrophobic to me. "Where'd you see him at Christmas?"

"My girl, Mary, she's really a good person. We went to her place the last couple of Christmases. She's Italian, so family's a big thing, and she makes me invite him. He never came before, but this year he did. Maybe it was because he was going to church or something."

"Did he come alone?"

"He brought a girl with him."

"What's her name?"

"I think it was Katy or something."

"Do you know where she lives?"

"No, but she was a waitress at Blueberry over on 41."

"Do you know Brett Tinder? He lives less than a mile away."

"Tinder? Nah, I don't think so."

I held up pictures. "How about Joe Chapman or Dick Cornwall?"

"Nope."

"Do you know if your brother was gay?"

"Gay? What are you talking about? What are you gonna tell me, besides being a crook, he was queer?"

"It's only a question about his orientation. We're trying to check connections between the killings we're investigating."

We finished up and left to follow-up on the only piece he gave that was worth following—a waitress at a diner.

<hr />

NOT BIG ON going out for breakfast, I'd never been to Blueberry. Like its name, the exterior was cute, but the inside, with its pine walls and knickknacks, screamed a place in upstate New York forty years past its prime. It didn't seem to matter, though. The place was nearly full.

I asked the hostess about Katy, assuring her it wasn't her we were interested in. Waiting on the porch, the smell of pancakes made my stomach growl. Two minutes later, the screen door swung open and a woman, not quite overweight or out of shape, but on the verge of both, came out. I tried to match the color from the hairs found on the victim to her hair.

"Hi. I'm Katy. You here about Shaun?"

"Yes. We understand you two were together."

"We were, but it ended a couple of months ago."

That was a good sign. I wasn't passing judgment on the fact she dated a criminal, but I was just glad it wasn't her hair. We still had a shot at finding if it belonged to the killer.

"You haven't seen him in a long while?"

"He came around a couple of times, saying that he'd changed and was straight. He even said he was involved at a church. But I'd heard that from him a dozen times before. I couldn't waste any more time with him. He was sweet, but as you know, he had a dark side. Maybe it was losing his mother early or something."

She came up for air, and I said, "He said he was going to church?"

"That's what he said."

"What church was that?"

"The Spirit, or something like that. It's all the way up Immokalee, out by Oil Well Road."

I asked, "The Spirit of Fellowship Church?"

"Maybe. I don't remember anything but the Spirit part, you know, the Holy Ghost?"

"Any mention of who the minister was? Was it Gabriel Booth?"

"I donno. I'm sorry."

Vargas asked, "Did he ever mention anything about being in danger? Or having enemies?"

She sighed. "Like I said, Shaun had a real sweet side to him, but he could only be good so long. I'm from a good family. My uncle is a cop up in Indiana, and, well, I knew he was up to no good. He'd hide out sometimes for days. It wasn't good. He probably had lots of enemies."

"How long were you together?"

"Less than six months."

I handed her my card, asking her to call with anything she thought could be helpful.

As soon as we got back in the car, I told Vargas to find out what other churches were out by Oil Well Road. As Vargas tapped on her phone, I said, "This could be the break we need to keep Chester off the top step of the dugout."

"Maybe, but there's two other churches out there, and one of them is The Holy Spirit Episcopalian Church, right on Oil Well."

Tony Kelp's apartment took up half the floor. I thought it was cool that the elevator opened right into his apartment, but the view was crazy. Squinting, I walked toward a bank of sliders that looked out on the shimmering Gulf. The fencing on the deck was done right—see-through—some sort of plexiglass.

"This is some view, Mr. Kelp."

"Every time I bitch about having to park underneath and take an elevator up with my stuff, I remind myself about the view."

I turned around, and as my eyes adjusted, said, "Seems like a good trade-off to me. How are you feeling?"

"Pretty good. It was a scare, but I'm lucky it was only the appendix. At my age, you feel pain, and your mind tells you this is it."

I didn't want to go down that path with him. "Well, you look good. Now, I'd like to ask you about the body found out there." It was my first time interviewing someone with the crime scene laid out below. "Tell me what you heard and saw that night."

"Sure, let's sit. You want something to drink?"

"You know what, I could use a water."

Kelp slipped around a black marble island to a stainless-steel fridge, and I glanced around. I was sure he was a widower based on the photos and furnishings, which had been dragged from his previous home. The heavy, Tuscan-inspired furnishings clashed with the Miami vibe of the high-rise. This place was worth a couple of million, and calling it an apartment or condo was a disservice.

I wasn't expecting a Pellegrino, and Kelp didn't disappoint, putting a bottle of Poland Springs on a Tommy Bahama coaster.

Twisting the cap, I said, "Thanks. So tell me what you remember."

"I get up a lot during the night to piss. You're too young yet, but you'll see."

He should only know my pee-pee problems.

"Anyway, I took a piss and climbed back into bed when I heard this noise. I was sure it a gunshot. It was a like a crack."

"It was late, and you'd been sleeping. I'm not doubting what you heard, but are you sure?"

"I served in the Korean War, and I know the sound of a firearm."

"I'm sure you do. I'm just trying to be certain. Would you know the difference in the sound between a rifle and handgun?"

"Years ago, when I was on the Korean Peninsula, I could tell you the difference between an M-16 and an M-19. I probably couldn't today, but I've got no doubt it was a handgun. The rest of me may be falling apart, but my hearing never fails me."

"Good, that's helpful. What did you do after hearing the gun fire?"

"When I heard the shot, I got up and looked out the window. There was a car—come here, I'll show you."

Kelp grabbed the cocktail table, pulling himself off the couch. He slid open a door to the deck, and we were engulfed by a humid, salt-laced breeze.

"I came out the bedroom door. It's one big deck. And there was this car." Kelp pointed to where Vanderbilt Drive crossed Wiggins Pass. "Sitting right there."

"Did you see anybody?"

"No, but the car was one of those Japanese types, and it had like strange lights on the back."

"What do you mean, strange?"

"It started moving, going north, but one side of the tail-lights looked like the reverse lights were on. You know, the white ones that come on when you back up?"

I nodded. "You sure about that?"

"That's what it looked like to me."

"You said the car was Japanese. How'd you know that?"

Kelp tugged an earlobe. "Japanese cars all make that whiny sound, really different from the sound American or European cars make. Jap cars make a burring sound, not aggressive sounding at all."

"Any idea on the make?"

"I'm really not sure; most of them look the same. You ever see the logos for Mazda, Infinity, and Lexus? They all look the same."

I had to agree. "You mind if we look through a couple of pictures, see if you can recognize the make of the car you saw?"

"Sure, no problem."

We cycled through most models, and though he leaned toward a Honda Accord, he wasn't certain.

16

———

Opening the car door, I heard my name called out. Vargas and I turned around. It was a secretary from the second floor.

"Sheriff wants to see both of you."

I said, "Tell him we're on the way to see a suspect."

"He said he wants to see you now."

"But—"

"Come on, Frank. Let's get this over with."

As we headed back in, I said, "It may be over for good."

"Stop with the end of the world stuff, okay?"

There were four coffee cups on Chester's desk and a stack of newspapers. The sheriff was on the phone. We stood behind the chairs in front of his desk as he finished the call. He motioned to sit but didn't get up.

"Take a seat."

Chester silently thumbed through a file marked FBI. I felt like a reliever who'd walked with the bases loaded and was waiting for the hook.

He flipped the file closed and tapped his forefinger on the stack of newspapers.

"I'd like you to tell me how we're going to regain the public's trust. It took years to build the relationships we have with the communities in our county, and this case threatens to destroy that sacred trust."

Vargas said, "It's been a difficult case, sir. This bad guy or girl has been careful, but we have several leads we're working."

"They better be strong ones."

Vargas said, "In fact, we were on our way to talk to our first real suspect when you called us in."

"What do you have on him?"

She said, "A friend of two of the victims said a man, Mike Moler, had made threats to both men. Moler has two priors— assault, and arrest for carrying a firearm."

Chester nodded. "He sounds interesting."

I said, "And we're working a line that this may be a hate crime. Two of the victims were gay."

"What about the others?"

"Not openly, sir. But we're probing."

"I assume both of you realize the pressure on my office is growing."

We nodded.

"Don't misunderstand this as a threat, but the clock is ticking."

WE LET the Lee County Police know we were going to Moler's, turning down their offer of help. The captain wasn't happy and said he'd have a squad car patrol in the East Terry Street area if we needed help.

I hesitated to say Mike Moler lived in a cinder-block cube, because with plywood covering both front windows, it looked more like a place you would squat in. The gravel walkway led to a door without a bell. I pounded a palm on the door several times before a runt of a man, with several days' worth of beard growth, opened the door.

"What the fuck you want?"

Vargas said, "We're with the Collier Sheriff's Office."

He narrowed his eyes. "What do you want?"

Moler was no more than five feet one and a hundred and thirty pounds. He was considerably smaller than all the victims. I'd run into a lot of small men who tried to supplement their stature with a gun.

"We're here to question you about some friends of yours."

"Who?"

"Joseph Chapman and Brett Tinder."

"What about 'em?"

"They were both murdered."

"So I hear."

Vargas said, "It might be better if we came in."

"I ain't letting you in without a warrant."

I said, "Mr. Moler, we can do this down at the station if you prefer."

"Ask your fucking questions right here. Okay?"

"How did you know them?"

He sucked in through his nose and spit just to Mary Ann's right. I wanted to kick this guy's ass all the way to Tampa.

"From work."

"Oh, we have to add stealing to your resume?"

He drew the back of his hand over his mouth. "You a funny man? I worked at the body shop, and they used to hang out there."

"What's the name of the place?"

"Collision Masters."

"Is that where you threatened to kill Chapman?"

"What are you talking about?"

"We have a witness who said that you got into a brawl with Chapman."

"Motherfucker deserved it. Fucking queer was one bossy mother jumper."

"So, you put him in his place?"

He shrugged.

"We heard Tinder jumped in, and they pinned you down, took your knife."

"Fucking fairies, both of them."

"You still work at Collision Masters?"

He stared at his feet. "Nah, been a while."

"How you make a living these days?"

"This and that."

"Do you own a firearm, Mr. Moler?"

He hesitated. "No."

"You own a car?"

He shook his head.

"How do you get around?"

"My girl's got a car."

"What make?"

"A Honda."

"What color is her hair?"

"Her hair? What the fuck does that have to do with anything?"

Vargas said, "Please, just answer the question."

"Dirty blond."

Afraid of tipping Moler off, I asked a couple of bullshit questions, and Vargas never missed a beat. We really made a good team, and I wondered if our personal relationship would screw things up before we thanked him for his time and left.

As soon as the door closed, I said, "We got to get inside. Let's draft a subpoena request."

"It'd be good to go for the car, even if it's not his."

"This is gonna be a tough sell as it is. We're gonna need Chester to push the DA."

"I doubt that's going to be a problem."

"Hope not."

"You know, Frank, you better be careful with what you say to the sheriff."

"What do you mean?"

"You misled him with the gay angle."

I shrugged. "It seemed like there was a connection until it petered out."

"It's dangerous telling him about a lead that we already dismissed."

"Aw, come on. Just buying a little time. I can resurrect it if needed."

"He finds out you're feeding him nonsense, you won't have to worry about being taken off this case."

"Don't worry, I'll handle Chester."

"I hope so."

"You still okay with me moving into the cabana?"

"I've told you a hundred times, it's fine. It could be fun."

It was too early in the relationship to be so close, but with this case I had no time to find a place to live. Truth was, I had banked on using her place and hadn't looked at anything for a while.

"Thanks. I really appreciate it. The movers are set to do it the day after tomorrow."

"Who'd you get to do the move?"

"A nephew of Candy's, in HR. Kid has a small moving company."

"Candy? Didn't you used to date her?"

"That was ages ago. Way before I got sick."

17

———————

It always seemed to happen to me. If I only had one important obligation, another one would be scheduled on the same day. Today was no different.

The sheriff was able to convince the DA to seek a search warrant of Moler's place. The judge signed it at 11:15. It was a big win, but I planned to take the afternoon off; the movers were coming to my place at one.

Vargas was waiting in the parking lot with two squad cars. Clutching the search warrant, I bounded down the stairs to meet them. I held the warrant in the air.

"Let's roll."

We sped down Livingston, and when we crossed over Bonita Springs Road it hit me.

"Shit!"

"What's the matter, Frank?"

"I forgot to notify Lee County we're executing a search."

"No problem. I called it in already."

"You did?"

"Yep. I called the Lee County Sheriff about our search warrant."

She really had my back.

"Thanks, I forgot all about it. Guess I was too excited about it."

Was I having another bout of chemo brain? I couldn't remember things. Mary Ann said I had too much going on with the case and finding a place to live.

"Shit!"

"What now, Frank?"

I hated admitting it, but the words just tumbled out. "I forgot to call the movers."

Vargas hesitated. "It's okay. What's the number? I'll see if they can do it around five. We should be done way before that."

"I donno. We may have to do interviews if we can nail Moler."

"It'll take a day or two for forensics to support an arrest."

"My stuff will be out on the street by then."

"We'll get it done. Even if we have to rent a U-Haul and do it ourselves."

Remembering how my ex-wife and I used a U-Haul when we moved in together caused my stomach to lurch.

Turning onto East Terry I saw two Lee County Police cars. They were parked just a few doors away from Moler's.

"What the hell are they doing here?"

"It's their territory, Frank."

"I don't want Moler spooked. He sees the cars, and he'll try to destroy any evidence."

"Take it easy. They're not out front. Besides, you forget the wood on the windows?"

Some kid was practicing the guitar next door as the door swung open.

Moler, in shorts and a tee shirt, looked like he'd been

sleeping. His hair was flattened on one side, and he had what looked like crud from drool on the side of his chin.

"What the fuck you want?"

About to present our search warrant, my hand stopped midair when I got a whiff of his alcoholic breath.

"This is a warrant. We're here to execute a search of your place. Step aside."

Moler swiveled his head. "What?"

Maybe it was the alcohol, but he genuinely seemed surprised.

Two uniformed officers stepped forward and escorted Moler to the carport at the end of the building. The apartment had only three rooms and had a neglected feel to it; dishes were piled in the sink and clothing was scattered around.

And there was a smell. The smell of a man living alone. It was the main reason I kept my place clean and organized. Shaking my head, I headed to the bedroom, and Vargas went to the kitchen.

A ceiling fan was spinning like it was attached to a fighter jet and clothing was strewn over a bed with no headboard. I dug out my gloves. A chest of drawers, capped by a dusty mirror, was the only other piece of furniture in the room.

Moler's phone, wallet, keys, an empty bottle of beer, and a couple of comic books covered the top of the dresser. I looked through his wallet. There was a photo of a blond woman. Was this his girl? The color of her hair was close to the hairs we'd found on Parker.

There was nothing else of interest in his wallet. I bagged the cell phone, hoping for connections, and moved to the drawers.

The bottom drawer was crammed with sweatshirts and pants, none of it folded. The next drawer contained socks, bathing suits, and shorts. As soon as I opened the third drawer

I noticed the edge of a plastic bag. Moving a tee shirt aside, I saw it contained marijuana. I took a photo and bagged the weed.

The top drawer had an assortment of underwear, coins, and paperwork. I shuffled through the documents: a copy of the lease for the place, and a self-storage receipt. I studied the receipt from Simply Self Storage. It was for a small five-by-five-foot unit. It had possibilities. Who knew what someone like Moler could hide there?

Sliding open a pair of bifold doors, verging on becoming unhinged, exposed a crammed closet. There were a couple of sundresses, skirts, and blouses hanging to the right of Moler's jeans. I patted pockets but came up with nothing. I slid three overflowing cartons on the closet's floor into the bedroom.

One was filled with pictures and memorabilia from Moler's family. I looked at a picture of a ten-year-old Moler standing in front of his parents. I studied the parents. The old man and the mother both had a drunkard's look to them. Moler never had a chance.

I pawed through a box topped with an old baseball glove. Below it was an ancient toolbox I'd bet was his father's and assorted junk you'd normally keep in a garage.

The last box had a tattered backpack containing swamp waders. I tossed it aside, and lying at the bottom was a partially empty box of shotgun shells next to a fishing reel. The 12-gauge shells contained shot used to hunt pheasants or turkeys. It wasn't worth making an issue of.

Before I left, I shut the fan and stood on the bed. The ceiling vent had been painted over. There was nothing hidden behind it.

The bathroom separated the bedroom and kitchen. I asked Vargas, "Anything?"

"Nope. What did you get?"

Waving the bags with the pot and cell phone, I said, "Moler's got a small self-storage unit at Simply. No telling what's in it."

I stepped into the yellow-tiled bathroom. An open bottle of Excedrin was on the sink. I flipped open the medicine cabinet: Band-Aids, a razor, hydrogen peroxide, toothbrush, and female deodorant.

Sliding the sunburst shower curtain aside, I swiped my forefinger over the drain. A blond hair was trapped by soap scum. I spied another blond hair stuck to a tile and bagged it as well.

A brown, faux leather couch anchored the family room. Its better days were when I'd been in high school. Opposite the couch was an old entertainment hutch that held a big tube TV. I strained my back getting behind the TV, but all I got for the effort was a handful of dust.

We left Moler's with our hopes resting on the cell phone and the storage unit.

18

Despite the experience, moving wasn't getting easier; it was getting old. Moving down to Naples a couple of years ago, the excitement of starting over was the fuel I ran on. I'd left my wife the furniture, but as we know, we accumulate a lot of crap besides furnishings.

Renting a furnished place gave me time to find a place and buy new furniture. Boy, was I glad I didn't take anything down from Jersey; it wouldn't fit in. But moving my boxes, organizing the deliveries, and unpacking, all while starting a new job, was challenging.

Even though I'd made a couple of runs last week, my car was still packed with clothes and bathroom stuff. The movers were loading the last piece, a coffee table, onto the truck headed for self-storage when I realized I'd have to turn the keys over.

This felt big, and I immediately regretted dragging my feet in looking for a place. It was risky. I wanted things to work out with Mary Ann, but being so close could screw things up. We'd have to work hard at keeping some distance. But how? The place had no kitchen, and if I picked something up without asking her, would she get pissed? And what about shopping? Shit, Luca, you boxed yourself in.

Punching a fist into my palm, I jammed the keys in a pocket, took one last look at my old place and jumped in my car.

SIMPLY SELF STORAGE was housed in a beige building on Airport Polling Road next to a CVS. The only thing distinctive about it was its lime-colored, metal roof. I swung around back where Sergeant Towbin and two uniforms were searching Moler's unit.

Getting out of my car, Towbin said, "Luca? What are you doing here?"

"Movers finished loading my stuff earlier than expected. What did you find?"

Towbin shook his head. "Nothing."

I surveyed the boxes that had been taken out of the square space. "You shitting me?"

"Nah, we're almost done—nothing here but family memorabilia—photo albums up the wazoo, a shitload of knickknacks, the usual crap people can't seem to get rid of."

Memorabilia? Moler was sentimental? I'd really seen it all. I pawed through a couple of boxes before heading over to my new living arrangement.

THE CABANA DOOR WAS OPEN, and I was looking under the bed when Mary Ann came in.

"You need some help?"

"I don't know where the hell I'm gonna put all this. Maybe I could get those plastic bins that fit under the bed."

"There's room in the spare bedroom's dresser. If you want, you can put your seasonal clothes in there."

"Thanks, but I got it under control."

"Okay, I'll be inside if you need anything."

Mary Ann wasn't the type to blackmail me, but I still felt uncomfortable handing over some of my independence. I was used to living alone the last couple of years, and though we weren't moving in together, you couldn't get any closer.

Her house had a long driveway with a garage to the right of the front door. A covered walkway from the house led to the cabana I was calling home. With its own entrance, it was ideal, if I didn't feel like it might cramp my style.

We'd agreed that I'd pay fifteen hundred a month, which would include utilities. But the last couple of days or so, Mary Ann said she didn't want any money. She felt funny, as the room was empty, and how much water and electricity was I going to use anyway. We argued about it, and in the end, I insisted on paying my way, or I'd move into a short-term rental.

Feeling like the whole thing was another huge lapse in judgment, I thought over my new living arrangements. Recalling my vow to take my laundry out to be done, get a microwave, and keep the tiny fridge stocked calmed me. What was I worried about? I'm forty-two years old, I know how to handle things.

Stacking three duffel bags under the window, I caught a glimpse of Mary Ann walking through the cabana's door. She was holding two glasses of wine.

"Welcome to the neighborhood."

MY PHONE SOUNDED its pee-pee alarm. It was the second time it went off. I threw the covers off and froze. Shit, what did I do? Screw up the first damn night? Sliding out of bed, I tried not to wake Mary Ann.

Following the night-light, I sat on the bowl. What's wrong with you, Luca? You threw the bullshit about keeping things the way there were but couldn't control your instincts for one night. Worse, tomorrow was a big day, and we had to be the same team we always were.

My pee came faster than usual. She had one of those newer toilets where the cover hid the seat, different from the one in the cabana. It stood higher, and I wondered if that made it easier for me.

Mary Ann rolled over, touching my arm as I got back into bed. I shifted from beating myself up to thinking about our meeting tomorrow. Sheriff Chester wanted to see us first thing in the morning. I tried to fall back to sleep, but the thought I'd be pulled off the case had me worked up. What else could it be that would have made his office call me after nine last night?

Mary Ann said I was letting my mind run away, that it was probably nothing. She was too much of an optimist. I tried to look at other possibilities, but I could sense bad news like an arthritic predicted the rain.

We were closing in. I wasn't going to be taken off the case without a fight. Three of the four suspects were connected to The Spirit of Fellowship Church. That kind of connection couldn't be ignored. How many members were there anyway? What were the odds that three end up murdered?

I thought about finding an excuse to miss the meeting, and next thing I knew, the alarm sounded and Mary Ann got out of bed.

19

———————

WHEN WE WERE SHOWN INTO SHERIFF CHESTER'S OFFICE, MY defenses shot up. He was behind his desk talking, a little too comfortably, with FBI Agent Haines. Chester rose and said, "Everyone here knows each other."

Vargas and I shook hands with Haines, who looked uncomfortable.

Chester said, "It's my feeling that we haven't worked close enough together. We could make real progress if we made full use of the resources the FBI have at their disposal."

My face was heating up. I wanted to tell him to fuck off, but I needed my job and kept quiet. The sheriff continued, "How many serial killing cases have you worked on, Agent Haines?"

He shuffled his stance. "Uhm, I don't know, a dozen or so."

"Well, unfortunately, we don't have any experience, right?" The sheriff looked at Mary Ann and me, and we nodded.

"I'm assigning Agent Haines a more active role in the investigation."

I said, "With all due respect to Agent Haines, I don't think that's necessary at this stage, sir."

"At this stage? You mean the stage with four bodies in the morgue? With the public frightened about their safety? With the governor breathing down my neck?"

With Haines staring at his feet, I said, "I realize it's a tough situation, but we've got a line we believe will lead us to the killer."

"That's good to hear. Now, why don't the three of you go down to your office and get this case closed."

Chester turned toward his desk, and just like that, I'd been demoted. I loosened my collar. My face burning, I headed to the bathroom to calm down.

Minister Booth was meeting with members of the church council, and it was running late. I put down the *Christian Monthly* I'd been paging through and stood.

"Vargas, I'll be right back. I'm gonna go ask his secretary about Parker, save us some time."

Approaching the church secretary, I asked, "Miriam, could you do us a favor while we're waiting for Minister Booth?"

"Sure, what do you need?"

"Can you check and see if a Shaun Parker was a member here."

"Oh yes. It was terrible what happened to him. It's so frightening."

"He was a member?"

"Yes. I'm sorry to say."

"Okay. What about Joseph Chapman? Was he a member?"

"Chapman? Hmm. Let me check." She tapped on her keyboard. "Oh yes, here he is, Joseph Chapman. Lives on 104th Street, not too far from here."

"Thank you."

Whispering, I said, "Parker was a member and guess who else? Chapman."

"Chapman? I thought the minister's wife said he wasn't."

"She did, and the question is, why would she say that? What's she hiding?"

The minister's office door swung open. Two women and a man said their goodbyes, leaving a smiling Gabriel Booth in the doorframe.

"Hello, Detective, sorry things ran later than expected."

"No problem. This is my partner, Detective Vargas."

"It's nice to meet you, Ms. Vargas, though I wished the circumstances were different. Come on in. Can I get you anything?"

We declined and took seats. The candle burning this time was cinnamon scented.

"I'm afraid we've got some bad news, Minister."

Booth's smile disappeared as he fell into his chair.

"There was another body found off of Santa Barbara, and the victim, one Shaun Parker, was also a member of your congregation."

The minister's face paled. "Oh my God. That's terrible news. I knew Shaun. Poor boy, he was so full of life. He had some difficulties but was on the right track."

Difficulties? Is that what church people call being a criminal?

"You may be aware, Mr. Parker had a long criminal record, like the other victims."

"As we discussed the last time, our ministry serves many who have strayed from God's plan, people who haven't followed his word but who have come here in a genuine attempt to get right with the Lord."

Vargas said, "That's admirable work, Minister Booth, and it's along those lines that we'd like to explore."

"I, I don't understand."

"Given the victims' backgrounds and their association with your church, we're going to have to take an in-depth look at the relationships—"

"You're not suggesting that the killer is connected to The Spirit of Fellowship, are you?"

Vargas said, "It's something we have to take a close look at. There is no way to ignore the connection."

"But how is this going to look? I realize you have to investigate, but I'm concerned about how this will appear."

I said, "I understand your concerns, Minister. We'll do this as discreetly as possible. I promise, if there are leaks, it will not come from our side. However, people, well, they like to talk. Bottom line is, we must examine the connection to the church and either clear the church or . . ." I let my voice trail off.

"Okay, okay, I understand. How can we help you?"

Vargas said, "We need to know how the church operates —what functions and services you deliver, how you recruit members, the organizational chart, that sort of thing."

I said, "We'll need to speak privately with your managers, the council, your wife—"

"Hannah? Why?"

Why was he questioning her participation? "She's an important part of The Spirit of Fellowship, isn't she?"

"Why, yes. But . . . let me speak with her first, okay?"

"That's fine, but time is of the essence—there's a killer on the loose."

Booth's face turned corpse gray.

Vargas said, "How about we start with you telling us about the activities the church is involved in?"

"We call our activities and outreach programs ministries. As the church has grown, so has the depth and number of ministries we operate. But behind it all is faith. The core of The Spirit of Fellowship is faith."

Booth was moving his hands like he was conducting an orchestra. "Spreading the Good News is central to what we do here and is the largest function of the church. We break the faith ministry into two broad categories, internal, how we educate our congregation, and our outreach program, where we reach out to the community at large and spread the Gospel."

Vargas asked, "Where do you go, physically, in the community?"

"Anywhere they'll have us." Booth laughed. "Seriously, we put a lot of effort into youth programs, elder outreach, addiction, prisons, the migrant workers, the Latino community."

"Who manages the various community efforts?"

Booth told us the names of the lieutenants involved and we moved on. It was a long list, including bereavement, a food bank, employment help, clothing drives, and an effort to help pay utility bills for those who fell on hard times.

It took us an hour to go through it all, and when we left I was convinced we should focus on the people involved in their outreach efforts, as well as his wife, Hannah.

20

Vargas and I waited at one of twenty round tables that filled the church's all-purpose room. I was speculating what the raised platform was for when a man with a crew cut entered. His tight shirt highlighted his muscles, making me suck my gut in. He flashed the slimmest of smiles and said, "I'm Jeremy Stokes. Minister Booth said you wanted to talk with me?"

Vargas said, "Thanks for taking the time. We'll try to be brief."

We shook hands, and he sat two seats away from Vargas. Putting an elbow on the table, his grapefruit-sized bicep expanded. Was he trying to impress her?

"So, what's up?"

I said, "What's up is we have four bodies in the morgue, and every one of them attended this church."

"It's a coincidence. We have almost four thousand members, you know."

"Coincidence? In my business there aren't coincidences. We call it evidence."

"Evidence? How so?"

Vargas said, "What Detective Luca and I are interested in exploring is any connection the killer may have with the church."

Stokes leaned in. "You really think this Aquatic Assassin character is a member of our church?"

Vargas said, "He or she may be a member or could be connected through one of your ministries."

I said, "Let's not forget, you appear to attract a lot of members who seem to have trouble staying out of trouble."

Stokes narrowed his eyes. "In case you didn't know it, Detective, we're all sinners. The Spirit of Fellowship is here to pick up those who have fallen and strengthen them with the word of God." He rapped his knuckles on the table. "You know, people deserve second chances."

This guy had his eyes closed. I had no problem with second chances, but the corpses were all habitual offenders. Some with ten or eleven chances.

I said, "Minister Booth called you his right-hand man. What are your duties at the church?"

"Basically, everything, though I try to focus on making sure the members who need support get what they need."

Vargas said, "Can you explain that?"

Stokes sighed. "People get in trouble, whether it be with the law, their personal life, alcohol, drugs, you name it. We're here as a support system for them. Basically, they stumble, we're there to pick them up."

Vargas said, "Say someone is on the road to recovery but relapses—you're there to help?"

Stokes nodded. "Recovery is never a straight line."

I said, "Considering the victims were all seasoned, uh, lawbreakers, if someone like them was arrested again, what would you do, bail them out?"

A vein on Stokes's temple began pulsing. "We'd make sure they had a roof over their head, something to eat, and try to find them a job."

"Very nice. I'm wondering why someone like you would do this type of work. Were you ever in prison?"

Stokes hesitated. "No, I do what I do for God. In Matthew 25:40, Jesus tells us that 'what you do for the least of these my brothers, you do to me.'"

How could they recite these passages without hesitation? They were like the people who worked at the Ritz. Maybe the Ritz recruited from the evangelical community. Was I impressed because my memory was chemo weakened?

I heard Vargas ask, "In your position you must have known all the victims."

"Yeah, I knew them. Uh, well, three of them anyway."

"Which ones?"

Another nanosecond of hesitation. "Chapman, Tinder, and Parker."

"When was the last time you saw Joseph Chapman?"

"I don't know, day or so before he went missing."

"What about Brett Tinder?"

"Probably the same."

"What about Dick Cornwall?"

Vargas was good, sneaking the name in, but then again, she did learn from the best.

"Same."

"I thought you said you only knew three of them."

"So? I saw him around here."

"You knew who Dick Cornwall was?"

"Of course."

"But you said you didn't know him."

"I knew who he was but didn't know him."

Bill Clinton would be proud of Stoker.

For a church person, he sure was smug. We danced around with him until a pepper-haired man with a goatee came in.

"Oh, I'm sorry. I thought it was my turn. I'll wait outside."

I said, "That's fine. We're done with Mr. Stokes."

Stokes's face relaxed and he left the room without saying goodbye. I didn't like Stokes; he needed a follow-up.

Fiftyish, Nick Santangelo took the same chair as Stokes. Santangelo ran the charitable outreach programs for the church.

He said, "Do you really think someone from the church has committed the murders?"

Vargas said, "We're here trying to figure that out."

"That's scary."

I said, "We understand you run the charitable side of things here."

"Yes, more like the outreach programs we run for the Latino and migrant worker community. People tend to forget that just fifteen minutes outside of Naples there are people just scraping by. Our mission is to support them, make their lives better, any way we can."

"By bringing them food?"

"They actually eat pretty well, especially those that work in agriculture. But we help them navigate the maze of programs out there that they can draw upon, make sure their children are enrolled and doing well in school. Those types of things."

I asked, "Do you have any interaction with the prisons or those recently released?"

"No, that's Jeremy's area, the guy that was just in here. I share some of our resources with him, but he handles that population."

"Did you know the four men who were killed?"

"I knew them but not well. Like I said, Jeremy knew them pretty good, I suppose."

"He said he didn't know Dick Cornwall."

"Are you sure? I saw the two of them leaving together the day Dick was killed."

I leaned toward Santangelo. "Are you absolutely sure about that?"

"Yeah, Dick was helping me stock the food pantry, and Jeremy came in to get him, said they were going to be late or something."

"Where were they going?"

"I don't know. They didn't say."

Vargas asked, "You're sure it was Dick Cornwall and that it was the day he was murdered?"

"It would be hard to forget something like that."

"Thank you for your time today, Mr. Santangelo."

Vargas leaned over as he left. "We should drag Stokes down to the station right now."

"Nothing would give me more pleasure, but the minister's wife is up next."

"Come on, Frank. Just because she's an introvert doesn't make her a suspect."

Twenty minutes past the appointed time, Hannah Booth came into the room holding hands with her husband, who said, "We're sorry to keep you waiting, but something came up, I couldn't break away."

Vargas said, "No problem, but we'd like to speak with your wife alone."

"Alone? Why?"

"It's standard procedure when conducting an interview."

"Hannah is uncomfortable speaking with you alone."

I said, "She has nothing to be afraid of, if she has nothing to hide."

"Is my wife a suspect?"

Vargas said, "Please, Minister, this is a simple interview we use to collect information. It helps us to put together a picture of where the church fits in all this."

The minister turned to Hannah, who slightly shook her head. The minister said, "If you insist on speaking with her alone, we're going to ask that you contact our attorney."

They seemed to be hiding something, and I wanted to get whatever we could from them before they lawyered up. I put my hands up. "Whoa, take it easy, Minister Booth. This is not adversarial. We'll break procedure as a courtesy. No problem. Take a seat, and let's get this over with. Okay?"

Hannah leaned on her husband as she lowered herself into a chair.

"You want me to get the cushion?"

"It's okay. My back feels okay now that I'm sitting."

The minister sat and reached for his wife's hand as I asked, "How long have the two of you been married?"

The minister smiled. "Hannah and I just celebrated our seventh anniversary."

"Congrats. Any children?"

"None together. I have a daughter with my first wife, whom I lost to cancer a dozen years ago. She's a sophomore, up at Florida State."

Trying to break the ice with the arctic queen was going nowhere. "Good school. So, Mrs. Booth, if you recall, we were trying to determine if Joseph Chapman was a member of the church, and you said you would check with Miriam."

Hannah said, "I don't remember saying that."

"Minister Booth, you were there."

"I don't recall the discussion verbatim, but I remember your interest in finding out who was a member."

"Does your husband's recollection help you at all?"

Hannah shook her head. "No. It was a busy day and unsettling to see the police here."

"Why would our presence unsettle you?"

"When the police show up, it's never a good thing."

Why the hell did anyone innocent feel uncomfortable with the police around? We're sworn to serve and protect, for God's sake.

Vargas said, "I understand, but what I'm confused about is you said he wasn't a member of this church, and when we checked with Miriam she said you never even asked her about Chapman."

"Are you saying my wife is being untruthful?"

"We're trying to clarify why she said what she did."

I don't know what confused me more, the smile she gave or what she said next.

"I may have been confused. This is God's house, and the work we do here is on behalf of his children. Well . . . it . . . it's difficult to reconcile the killing of these young men."

"Do you know who might have killed these men?"

Minister Booth said, "Detective, if we knew we'd be the first to tell you."

"Mrs. Booth, when was the last time you saw Brett Tinder?"

There was a slight quiver to her lips as she said, "I don't remember."

"You don't remember?"

Minister Booth said, "My wife has a very bad back and the painkillers she takes can make her forgetful at times."

How convenient. "When did you see Dick Cornwall last?"

"I don't remember."

"Is there anything you do remember?"

Minister Booth said, "Detective, please, there is no reason to antagonize Hannah. We came here voluntarily to offer our assistance."

Hannah sniffled and turned to her husband. "Let's go. I want to leave."

21

The smell of nail polish hit me as I finished up a call. I hated it when Vargas touched up her nails in the office. I said, "Well, things just got a bit more interesting. Hannah Booth or Hannah Gilbey, as she was known when married to a John Gilbey, had a son who died ten years ago. The cause of death was listed as an overdose. But the coroner said he wasn't sure it was an overdose and wanted to conduct an autopsy. There were some markings on the kid's face that he thought might have come from smothering."

"What? Who found him?"

"Hannah. She said he was dead when she came back from grocery shopping."

"Why didn't they do an autopsy, if there was suspicion?"

"No one seems to know, but the kid was an addict who'd overdosed three times before."

"Maybe she put him out of his misery."

"Exactly what I'm thinking. If so, she's killed before."

"It'd be a stunner if she turned out to be the killer."

"You know, Vargas, nothing surprises me anymore."

"That's not a healthy perspective to see of the world, Frank. Cynicism is like acid."

"Okay, okay. What did you get on Stokes?"

"For starters, he served a stint, courtesy of Lee County, for assault with a deadly weapon. Beat some guy unconscious after cracking his head open with a bottle."

"I knew it! He still on probation?"

"No, it ended a year ago."

"What else?"

"Stokes and Cornwall knew each other good enough to have lunch together most days."

"Holy shit. So, the question is, why would Stokes lie about that and prison?"

"Maybe he bet that we wouldn't follow up on him."

"If that's what he was betting on, he should have been more cooperative."

"How you want to proceed? Should we bring them in?"

"I'd love to, but they'll probably demand attorneys."

"For sure."

"Let's go to them."

We headed down the hall to the parking lot. Vargas slammed into my back when I stopped short. Minister Booth was saying goodbye to the desk sergeant on his way out.

"What the hell was he doing here?"

Before Vargas could say anything, I got my answer from the sheriff's secretary.

"Glad I caught you. The sheriff wants to see you."

"Can it wait? We're heading out."

"He said now."

I stared at Chester's yellow tie as the sheriff told us to lay off the minister's wife. It was unfair, but I'd save my fight for when I had more than a few beads of information. I didn't mind keeping my mouth shut since we were allowed to pursue other church connections.

IT COULD HAVE BEEN AN ILLUSION, but Stokes's muscles seemed to have shrunk like his arrogance when we showed up at his office. Stokes knew the power had shifted with his losing bet. He jumped up when he saw us.

"Can this wait? I was about to leave."

I bet you were. "Nope. Sit down."

"But—" He fell back into his chair.

Vargas said, "When Detective Luca asked you if you were ever in prison, you said no. Why'd you lie?"

Stokes shrugged. "I was embarrassed. It was a long time ago. I made a mistake and paid the price."

I said, "What did you think, we weren't going to check up? You think we're stupid?"

"No, of course not. Like I said, I don't like talking about it."

"Lying to an officer is obstruction of justice. You want to go back in?"

"Come on, man. Give me a break, I should have been honest but—"

Vargas said, "You also claimed not to know Dick Cornwall."

Stokes's shoulders sunk. "I knew him. A lot of times we ate lunch together."

"Why'd you lie?"

"I was afraid. You know, with my record and knowing all the guys who got shot, that you'd look at me as a suspect."

"And what do you think we think now? You think you're any less a suspect now?"

"You got to believe me. I had nothing to do with any of that."

"Mr. Stokes, do you own a firearm?"

There was that hesitation again.

"I'm a convicted felon. It's against the law for me to have a gun."

His arrogance may have receded, but his Bill Clinton word parsing was in full flower.

I slammed a palm down. "Let's stop with the bullshit, okay? I don't care if you have a right to have a firearm or not. The question is, do you own one?"

Stokes frowned as he nodded. "There's been a couple of burglaries out where I live. I felt like I needed protection."

"What kind of firearm?"

"A Bodyguard, with the laser guide thing."

"What color is the laser?"

"Red."

For the first time he seemed to be telling the truth, unless he had other guns.

"Where were you the night of June twenty-fifth? The night Joseph Chapman was murdered."

"I was here until almost ten o'clock that night."

Vargas said, "That's rather late. What were you doing here at that hour?"

"We had a healing ceremony at around seven that night."

Vargas said, "What time did it end?"

"It went about an hour. We didn't get the turnout that Minister Booth hoped for, otherwise they can drag on for hours if a lot of people want a prayer team session."

Most people, including Mary Ann, would think I'd be a skeptic about a healing power coming from God through a minister or priest, but the fact was my mother took me to one when I was six years old. I was constantly getting ear infections that were so bad they began to affect my speech. The kids at school were taunting me about it.

My aunt told Mom that a priest from India, with a reputation for healing, was coming to our diocese.

It was snowing the night of the mass. Mom bundled me up and took me to St. Mary's in Middletown, NJ. I remember all the wheelchairs lining the aisle to the altar. Besides a couple of babies, I was the youngest there.

I heard Vargas say, "That leaves two hours unaccounted for."

"We ate dinner and hung around talking."

"Who's we?"

"Me and Dick Cornwall."

I wish I had a twenty for every time a suspect gave an alibi that included a dead man.

"Anyone else?"

"No, just us."

I said, "What did you eat?"

"Eat?"

"Yeah, what did you eat?"

"We got some Cuban food at Roma in Havana."

"But you said you ate here."

"We picked it up."

"You drove all the way there to do takeout?"

"It's no big deal. It's not that far."

"How did you pay for the food?"

"With cash. It was like fifteen bucks each."

"After you left the church, where did you go?"

"Home. It was getting late."

"Did you see Joseph Chapman at the healing service?"

"No, he wasn't there."

"Was Minister Booth and his wife there?"

"The minister was there but not Hannah."

Interesting. "I understand Mrs. Booth knew all the victims as well. Was she close with any of them?"

"Close? What do you mean by that?"

"That was a poor choice of words, I meant friendly."

"She pretty much keeps to herself, but she did have an argument with Chapman a couple of weeks ago."

"What about?"

"I don't really know the particulars, but Hannah and a couple others wanted changes in the way the place was run, and I guess Chapman disagreed, but I don't know for sure. But man, was she pissed. She was screaming at him and threw a hymn book at him."

"Anyone else see the fight?"

"Minister Booth was there, and so was Nicky Santangelo."

"Did Mrs. Booth have arguments with any of the other victims?"

"You're not— no, she can't be involved, she's—"

"I'm not saying anything, just asking if she had any disagreements with them."

"I don't really know."

My pee-pee alarm buzzed again. There was pressure in my abdomen. It was time to go. Besides, we were finished with Stokes for the time being. I told him to make sure he got rid of his gun and we left.

I knew there was a bathroom outside of the minister's office. Before heading for it, I asked Vargas to see if the Cuban restaurant Stokes said he went to had camera surveillance.

"You did what?"

"When I went to the bathroom, I was sitting there and saw a hairbrush on a shelf by the sink. It had to be hers. So, I took two pieces of hair off it."

I took a plastic evidence bag out of my pocket and showed Vargas.

"Frank, the sheriff told you to steer clear of her."

I smiled. "She was nowhere to be found."

"What are you going to do with it?"

"I'm gonna have forensics check and see if it's a match with the hair found on Shaun Parker."

"And if it is?"

"I'll take it to Chester."

"He's going to sanction you, Frank. You ignored a direct order. Why don't we give it to Haines?"

"What, and let him get the credit?"

"There you go again with your hero complex."

"It's not a complex. It's just not fair, that's all."

Vargas exhaled. "Let's see if it matches, first."

"Okay. Hey, that restaurant Stokes said he went to, they have video?"

"Yeah, I texted Boyle, told him to go down and pick it up."

"See if they have a parking lot feed. Stokes may not have gone in."

"They do. You know, Frank, sometimes I get the feeling you think I don't know what I'm doing."

"No, no. That's not true. You're a great detective." Chemo had impacted my memory, and I was looking for ways to prove it wasn't as bad as it really was.

"Thanks. Don't get all defensive on me, but you kinda zoned out there when Stokes was talking about the healing mass."

"It brought back a memory, that's all."

"You want to talk about it?"

"When I was about six, I had problems with my ears, and it started to mess with the way I talked."

"What was the problem?"

"Ear infections that would never go away. I was taking all kinds of antibiotics, but nothing worked. I became resistant to them. Anyway, my aunt told my mother about a priest who'd healed a lot of people. And this priest was coming to St. Mary's, which wasn't far away. I didn't really understand what it was all about, she just said he was able to channel God's power to help people that were sick."

"How come you never told me?"

"I don't know. I kinda buried it. As I got older I guess I thought it was a little ignorant or something."

"I believe in God's power. I never went to a healing mass, but I always wanted to. What happened?"

"The night we went it was snowing like crazy and freezing. I remember my mother driving really slowly, but it didn't stop anybody from coming. St. Mary's was jammed. Wheelchairs lined the aisle to the altar, but other than a couple of babies crying, there was nobody my age."

"You must have been frightened."

"Churches were always spooky to me as a kid, but that night there was a festive kinda feel. People were talking and praying in groups. Then the bells rang and everyone sat down. It started off like a regular mass and with Communion, but then the priest started praying out loud and people started shouting out names of people my mom said needed help. It went on for a while, and he went up and down the aisles sprinkling holy water on us."

"It must have been scary for you. I wish I had've been there."

"You know what? It wasn't, well, not all the time. I didn't

really know what was going on. But then the priest came off the altar and started to pray in a circle over each of the people in the wheelchairs. When I saw tears on my mother's face, though, I did get scared. My mother grabbed my hand and waited for the priest. She spoke to him, and the next thing I know, I'm with the priest in the middle of a group of people who were praying. It sounds crazy, but I began feeling dizzy, like I was going to fall. The priest put his fingers in my ears and kept praying, and the next thing I know I was crying."

"What an emotional experience. What happened?"

"We left. It had stopped snowing, which my mom said was a miracle. She kept asking if my hearing had changed. I couldn't tell the difference. She put the radio on, and I said it seemed to be a little better because I felt bad. The rest of the ride home we said the Rosary. The next morning when I woke up my hearing was noticeably better."

"Really? Are you playing with me, Frank?"

"No. I swear it's true. From that day on my hearing was better. I had a couple of infections after that, but they went away fast with the antibiotics."

"Oh my God. You experienced a miracle, Frank." Vargas gave my hand a squeeze.

"I guess so."

It was a hard thing to admit. There was no real proof. The doctors said I grew out of it, but Mom was resolute it was God answering her prayers. She went to mass every day for the rest of her short life. I should have tried a healing mass for my cancer, but when I got the news I couldn't think straight.

22

———

MY PHONE WAS VIBRATING; IT WAS THE REAL ESTATE LADY again. Her last message went on about the perfect house she'd found for me, imploring me to see it before it was snapped up by another buyer. Though prone to exaggeration, like all in sales, she was a nice lady who'd put up with my cancelations and particular preferences. She deserved a callback.

I'd really settled into Mary Ann's cabana. It was small, but that negative was a plus. Cleaning took minutes, and there was no place to collect stuff. Maybe there was something to this minimalist way of living. With a half-sized fridge, I never had to throw any food out.

It was carefree living, and the costs were low. Plus, there was no maintenance to suck up whatever free time I had. No guilt trips for spending a day on the sand instead of painting something.

The idea of parting with my savings and being hamstrung with a mortgage and a list of things to do lost its appeal. Why not invest the money in the stock market instead? Weren't there tons of millionaires who made their fortunes on Wall

Street? My savings should be growing instead of trying to fill the money pit known as a house.

"Marilyn, it's Frank Luca. All's good, but I've been swamped. I'm sure you've seen the news about the serial killer. Yeah, I'm the lead on the case." Though who knew for how long. "In Pelican Perch? Sounds really nice. What are the HOA fees like in there? Okay, your message said they were motivated sellers. Just how motivated are they? Did they move out? If they're moving next week, the pressure is going to build. Think we should wait a week or two?"

I hated when an agent said there were other buyers looking at the home. In a vibrant market, you'd expect that. "Let me get back to you after I get done here, and I'll see what my week looks like."

It was a three-bedroom home that, if the agent was truthful, did sound like something for me. Good location, new kitchen, and baths. I'd have to rip out the carpets, maybe put some hardwood in, but that was about it. It was priced right, at $635,000, after a fifty-grand reduction. Still, it was a lot of money to spend, and there was the five hundred dollar a month association fee to pay. Did I really need to move? Things were going pretty good with Mary Ann, and I had some space to myself. Why would I want to saddle myself with a house?

23

Vargas popped in the surveillance DVD from the Cuban restaurant and scrolled to an eight o'clock time stamp.

I said, "I'm starting to feel like we're on the wrong track with Stokes. He could've been with Cornwall at the restaurant and killed him after they ate. This doesn't help us."

"Let's look this over before we jump to any conclusions."

"Come on, Vargas, you know jumping to conclusions is an Olympic sport with me."

"That's Cornwall at the counter now. It's eight twenty-six."

The video feed was clear. "Yeah, that's him, but where's Stokes?"

"He's paying in cash, like Stokes said. And there's two bags."

As Cornwall exited, Vargas switched DVDs. The outdoor footage was dark and grainy. Vargas slowed it down, and we saw Cornwall leave the restaurant, walking toward a reddish-colored compact that was to the far right of the entrance.

"Cornwall had a Ford Focus, didn't he?"

"I think so." I pawed through the case file. "Yeah, a 2012 red Focus."

He opened the door and put the bags on the rear seat, then got into the driver's seat.

"I can't tell if anyone's in the passenger seat."

"Maybe when he backs out we'll get a view."

The car backed up and left the lot without a clue as to whether he was alone or not.

"Told you it was a waste of time. I can't believe the church doesn't have cameras."

"It's a church, Frank. God looks after it."

"Really? Well then, can you explain how the crucifix at Ave Maria disappeared?"

Vargas spoke in a whisper, "Ascension."

"Ascension. You really believe that?"

"Your hearing's pretty good, isn't it?"

"I'm not even going there. I'm going to see Stokes. You coming?"

Vargas checked her watch. "I'm due in court at eleven."

"McCuskey trial?"

"Yeah."

"I'll text you then."

"Okay, and remember to stay away from Hannah."

"What's the matter, you jealous?"

EVERY TIME a quick rainstorm passed through, I checked my watch. Maybe it had to do with the misconception it rained at three o'clock every summer day. Noting it was only ten forty-five, I pulled into the church's parking lot. The sun was out in full force and steam was rising from the pavement as I walked toward the church's office doorway.

When told Stokes was out with a stomach virus, I asked to see Nick Santangelo.

Santangelo's office was one of four that lined a hallway that ended with the minister's office. Santangelo's desk was filled with picture frames, and his credenza had a large candle burning, emitting a spicy scent.

Wearing a smile and a white shirt, Santangelo maneuvered around a stack of cartons containing Bibles, to greet me.

"Detective—"

"Luca, Frank Luca."

"Good to see you again. How's the investigation going?"

"I'd like to ask you some questions about an argument between Hannah Booth and Joseph Chapman."

Santangelo's face crumpled into a frown. "If you're suggesting that a simple disagreement led Mrs. Booth to murder Joe, you're way off track."

Dismissing the possibility out of hand showed how ignorant he was of the world I worked in. I guess he never read the papers either. "I'm not suggesting anything. Mr. Stokes claimed that both you and Minister Booth were present when an argument between Mrs. Booth and Chapman broke out. Is that true?"

"Yes. But it wasn't a big deal, Detective. There are a lot of disagreements in any organization."

"What was the argument about?"

"Some programs and the focus of the church's resources."

"Can you get more specific?"

"There are some people on the leadership council that feel some of our efforts are, let's say, a distraction and are pushing to eliminate certain outreach programs. Joe Chapman and Hannah were talking about it, and it got a little heated."

"I'd say throwing a book at someone qualifies for more than a little heated."

"We all lose our cool at times."

"Was Hannah Booth for the changes?"

"Yes, she's been pushing to refocus our efforts."

"You mentioned a leadership council. Who makes up this group?"

"Minister and Mrs. Booth, me, Stokes, Carol Black, Ester Pasquale, Ronnie Sales, and Marty Corbin."

I jotted down the names. "What was the nature of the change that resulted in the fight?"

"It wasn't a fight. Mrs. Booth was concerned, as others on the council have been, that we're spread too thinly. That we should reduce some programs, refocus our mission."

He said the same thing twice. What was he hiding? "What programs were going to be cut?"

"The financial support we offer to those battling addictions and those being released from jail."

It made sense in my book. Hannah and the others were tired of walking uphill. It was also natural that Chapman, a felon, would object. There probably was nothing more to the argument.

"With Hannah being the minister's wife, she'd be able to get the policy changes she wants."

He shook his head. "Not really. Minister Booth is a very compassionate man. He has the last word on what we do here, and I can tell you, he's pushing back at the attempts to curtail our outreach."

"How did the others feel about the proposed cuts?"

"I agreed with the minister and so did Carol and Ester."

"I'd guess Mrs. Booth's frustration got the better of her."

"Yeah, but I can tell you she wasn't alone. Ronnie and Marty got pretty vocal with the minister."

"Any Bible throwing?"

He smiled. "Fortunately, no."

"Tell me a little about the other men on the council."

"Marty's a little older but a great guy with an inspiring story. Minister Booth ran Bible classes at the prison, and Marty studied like mad, turning himself around. He was the first guy Minister Booth helped when he got out of jail, and that's what started the prison outreach program."

Every now and then you win one, but as a beneficiary of a program, why'd he want to shut it down?

"How old of a guy?"

"I think he's in his late sixties or so."

Checking my notes, I asked, "What about Ronnie Sales?"

Santangelo shrugged. "Not much to say. He's kinda quiet. I gotta be honest with you, he doesn't have much of a personality."

I cringed at 'I've got to be honest with you.' So, everything else people said before they invoked the stupid saying was bullshit?

"What's his role at the church?"

"He takes care of the books for the church and helps with outreach."

Was there a financial angle to the killing spree? Maybe an embezzlement scheme that got discovered and needed silencing?

"How are the church's finances?"

"I think okay, but I wouldn't really know."

"Why wouldn't you know? Doesn't the council have access to the church's finances?"

"Minister Booth and Ronnie handle all of that themselves."

24

———

Distracted by the voices from roll call, I shut our office door.

"You know, Vargas, the more I think about it, we got to drill down on the church's books. Maybe Booth is hiding something."

"You think so?"

"You know what I say, 'More people have been murdered over money than love.'"

Vargas crumpled a piece of paper and tossed it at me. "Thanks for reminding me. You do know that Minister Booth will probably go to the sheriff if you start asking about their finances."

"Why? It's a legitimate line of inquiry."

"Come on, Frank, it's circumstantial at best. How do you link any financial problems to the killings? That is, if the church even has a money problem."

"These churches are nonprofits, so I can't see how they can try and hide. Don't they have to file a return or report with the IRS?"

"I'd think so, but you know McDonald up in FCU. Why don't you go see him?"

"We're on the same wavelength, Vargas."

Embarrassed by my childish refusal to give her credit, I headed to the Financial Crimes Unit.

It was so quiet in the room where FCU operated, you'd have thought you weren't in a police station. I had thought the seven-person unit was large for a place with the population of Collier County. But there were quite a few heavy hitters in Naples and no shortage of scammers looking to separate them from their money.

FCU officers were more like accountants than cops, and there were more than their spreadsheets separating them from the frontliners. Other than McDonald, I'd barely spoken to anyone else in the room in the four years I'd been down here.

McDonald was a good ten years older and twenty pounds heavier than me. Like me, he'd also gone to John Jay but was a lot more ambitious, leaving with a double degree in law enforcement and forensic accounting. Maybe it was the fact he was originally from Queens that created a touch of a bond. He waved me over to his desk.

"How you doing, Frank?"

"Good, you?"

"All's well. What's going on?"

"It's early, but I'm working an angle on the Aquatic Assassin case. There seems to be a connection with a church called The Spirit of Fellowship, and I'm getting the vibe something may not be quite right with their books. I'd love to get my hands on whatever financial reports they put out."

"Well, you'd need a subpoena, and unless you have more than you're telling me, there isn't a judge around who'd sign one. You have anything concrete?"

My phone pinged, and I snuck a look. It was a text from

Vargas, 'Where are you?' Where am I? She knew I was up here.

"I wish I did. Any suggestions?"

"If they borrowed any money and the lender filed a lien, it'd be on file in the public domain."

I lowered my voice. "Can you run a search for a fellow John Jayer?"

"No problem."

"I owe you a brew."

I stepped back into the buzz of the station, and before I closed the door behind me, my phone rang.

"Vargas, what? are you getting dementia or something?"

"Get back to the office. There's a match on the hairs."

I took the stairs two at a time and ran into my office. Vargas picked up a forensics report and handed it to me.

"Holy shit, Vargas. This is huge. I'm telling you—when Luca's got a hunch, it's like gold in the bank."

"How are you gonna tell Chester you got the samples?"

My smile crumpled. "I'll just tell him."

"I don't think that's going to go over well."

"Why not? We've got her. Chester can't say shit."

"Hold on. We have her hair on a corpse—nothing more, nothing less."

"Let her explain how it got there, then."

"All I'm saying is, Chester is a stickler for the rules. He gave you a direct order that you ignored. You may win this one, but you're going to pay hell for it. I wouldn't put it past him to sanction you."

"That's bullshit, and you know it."

"I'm only telling you how I see it, Frank. I don't want you to pay a price for this."

I slammed my chair into the desk. "So, we got solid evidence, and I gotta keep it in the drawer?"

"Why don't we get Haines to help us out?"

"Haines? What—are you, crazy? You're nuts if you think he'd help us. He'd be riding in on a white horse."

Vargas exhaled loudly and headed for the door. "Would you listen to yourself? You sound like a five-year-old. Do what you want, okay?"

"Hold on, now. Take it easy, will you? If you think we should talk to Haines, then we will."

Haines was working out of the FBI field office on Gateway Boulevard in Fort Myers. There was no way I was going to him. Vargas read me like a card and said, "I'll give him a call and tell him we need to see him."

HAINES CAME DOWN from Fort Myers an hour after Vargas reached out. It was quicker than I expected, increasing my wariness. He was wearing a grin, and a dark blue suit, and greeted us like old friends.

"How are you guys doing?"

I said, "Grinding it out. How're things in the ivory tower?"

Vargas laughed nervously and shook Haines's hand, who said, "Tell you the truth, it's been boring. I've been going through satellite images of the crime scenes but getting nothing out of it. Plus, I'm starting to really miss my kid."

"Well, maybe we got something that's going to get you back home."

"What do you have?"

I handed him the forensic report. "The hairs found on the fourth body, Shaun Parker, are a match with Hannah Booth."

"The minister's wife?"

Vargas said, "Yep. Tough to believe, but there could be several reasons. Maybe she was having an affair with him."

"Come on, Vargas. You're reaching."

Haines said, "Doesn't seem to be any doubt they're hers. Most of the time, hair samples can be tricky, but both of these had more than enough of the follicles intact, and there was ample DNA collected. You want me to have the bureau's guys look it over?"

Vargas said, "No, the lab down here is top-notch. We're going to need some help with Chester."

"The sheriff?"

"Yeah. You see, when we started taking a look at the church, Frank focused on Hannah. The minister felt it was unfair and complained to Chester."

"And he backed off?"

"Yeah, at the time. It was nothing more than Frank's intuition."

I said, "Chester told me to stay away from her."

"It was a direct order."

"How'd you get a sample of her hair?"

"You see, I was at the church interviewing someone else, and I used the bathroom. I noticed a hairbrush, and the hairs on it were a color match."

Vargas said, "Chester's a good man, but he'll settle the score once this case is closed. Frank will pay a price for ignoring a direct order."

Haines cupped his chin with a palm. "First off, we've got to establish that the hair was hers without a doubt. We need an independent source of her DNA. I have no knowledge she is off-limits. Let me take a ride to see her under the guise of cross-checking the profile we've built. I'll find a way to get something with her DNA on it."

I didn't want him near Hannah, but before I could object, Vargas said, "Perfect. We'd really appreciate it."

"No problem. I'm here to help you nail this bad guy, or girl, as it may be. Once we can confirm the DNA match with the hairs on the victim, I'll go see Chester."

"You'd be some hero in his eyes."

"Nothing's getting solved with just the match, Frank. Besides, I'll tell him you kept whispering in my ear about her, and I took action based on your instincts, which, by the way, are damned good."

25

HAINES INFORMED SHERIFF CHESTER THAT THE DNA HE lifted from a water bottle Hannah Booth drank from matched the hairs found on the fourth corpse.

Chester steepled his fingers. "Interesting. If you don't mind, I'd like to know what made you even consider testing her?"

"It's the training, sir. We don't like to say it in public, but the bureau likes to treat everyone surrounding a crime as a suspect until cleared."

"Are you aware that I specifically ordered Hannah Booth to be off-limits?"

"Yes, sir. Detective Luca advised me to seek your permission beforehand, and I had every intention to do so, but seeking feedback on some of the associates of the church, the perfect opportunity arose to obtain a sample without upsetting anyone."

The room was getting too warm, and I reached to loosen my collar as Chester trained his eyes on me.

"Did either of you put Agent Haines up to this?"

"No, sir," rang out in stereo.

"Good. My order was an attempt to focus the investigation, and in no way was I trying to protect her. At this point, the directive is lifted, and Mrs. Booth has some explaining to do."

"We'll get to the bottom of this, sir."

"I don't have to tell you how urgent this is, do I?"

Haines said, "Everyone is aware of the urgency, sir, and if I may say so, you have yourself two very qualified detectives."

<hr>

MARY ANN and I took the same booth we always did when we went to Naples Flatbread. I wasn't a big fan of the food, but she loved their Southwestern salad. She ordered her usual, and I took a chance on a flatbread with figs on it.

Sipping an inexpensive Brunello, I said, "We have to tread carefully with the minister's wife. There's no doubt there's a connection between the church and the killings. But if it turns out that Hannah isn't it, we'll need allies inside the church."

"The file Haines sent down raises a bunch of questions, especially the suspicions on the death of her son."

"I kinda feel bad for her. It's gotta be hell to have a kid addicted to drugs."

"Look at you. Getting soft, are you?"

"No, seriously, can you imagine what these parents must go through? How the hell do they even sleep?"

"Total disaster; it must consume them."

"Maybe she did the kid in. Save both of them a shitload of misery."

"I don't know, Frank. A mother killing her own kid is super rare."

"Rare as an adult, but not unheard of."

A waitress with a tee shirt that read 'What the Flatbread?' delivered our food.

I picked up a piece of flatbread, and after trying to find a fig, said, "You remember the woman up in Charlotte County whose daughter was a prostitute? She ended up taking a shotgun to her and her pimp."

Mary Ann put her fork down. "Can we not talk about this while we're eating?"

"Sorry." I smiled and finished my slice. In search of my first fig, I picked up another piece. "You think this million-dollar loan the church took out has anything to do with anything?"

Mary Ann finished a forkful of salad and said, "Can I ask you something?"

"Sure."

"Is this a date, or not? Because if it's a date, I don't want to talk about work."

It wasn't easy, but I made it through dinner without mentioning the case. It got easier once we started walking around Mercato, where there were plenty of distractions to occupy my mind.

It was a tough call, but I decided to take a run at Hannah on her own turf. Even though her husband was sure to be there, I was hoping to get something before hauling her in, which would result in her getting a mouthpiece. Haines called the minister requesting a meeting under the guise we wanted information about two people connected to the church, insinuating they matched his profile.

Minister Booth stood, did a double take, looking over my

shoulder when Vargas and I were shown in. He rescued his smile and shook our hands.

"I was under the impression Agent Haines was coming."

"He was supposed to, but something came up in DC. He had to fly up this morning." It sounded like bullshit, even though it happened to be true.

"Oh, I hope it's nothing serious."

I scanned the top of his desk, and there were documents with the Fifth Third Bank's logo on them. McDonald said the loan was from Wells Fargo, what was this?

Vargas set her valise beside her chair and said, "He mentioned something about a case he was working on, said it was coming to a head."

Booth smiled. "The FBI always gets their man."

Before I got into law enforcement, I used to think the G-men were invincible. The truth is, they've got as many pimples as any other organization.

Vargas said, "Is your wife, Hannah, coming?"

"Yes, she'll be right in."

I said, "I couldn't help notice the papers from Fifth Third Bank. I use them as well. You ask me, they have the best customer service."

"We have our checking account with them. Oh, here she is."

Hannah's black jeans hugged her curves, and she topped off with a gray chiffon blouse. She was carrying a blue seat cushion, and her blond hair was pulled back in a ponytail, revealing earringless lobes. It could have been the lack of makeup, but her face seemed puffy and lined.

We stood, and she nodded in acknowledgment, snaking her way to a chair next to her husband.

Vargas said, "Before we begin, I'd like to thank both of you for making time for us."

Minister Booth reached for his wife's hand, saying, "We're always happy to help."

I said, "A connection with your church seems highly probable. With that in mind, Agent Haines believes there might be a financial aspect motivating the killer."

Booth said, "I don't understand. Can you elaborate?"

Vargas said, "How are the church's finances, Minister?"

"We're doing fine. It's always a challenge to raise the funding we need to execute our mission, but God always provides what we need."

I wanted to ask him if there was a Wells Fargo loan officer whose last name was God, but said, "Is it customary for the church to borrow money?"

Booth shifted in his chair. "From time to time we may need to take a small loan out."

"Do you consider a million dollars small?"

Hannah winced as she shot forward. "You have no right to ask these types of questions."

"My wife is right. I don't see the point, Detective. Just what are you inferring?"

Vargas said, "Agent Haines thought it was possible that someone may have been embezzling money from the church. The scheme may have been discovered, and to cover it up, he or she had to resort to killing."

Hannah narrowed her eyes as Booth said, "This sounds like a Hollywood movie."

I said, "Who handles the finances for the church?"

Booth said, "It's my responsibility to safeguard the resources we receive, and I take it very seriously. The thought someone might steal from us, steal from God, is impossible to comprehend."

Was he really that ignorant, or was something going on here? We'd have to nose around before we pushed him any further. "Does anyone help you manage the resources; maybe your wife?"

"Hannah has enough to do around here, but thank God for Ronnie Sales. He's very good with numbers."

I'd arrested quite a few mathemagicians when I was up in Jersey and asked, "Who receives the statements from the bank?"

"We get them here, at the office."

"Do you review them before anyone else, before Mr. Sales sees them?"

"The seminary stressed, no, actually drilled it into us, the importance of independent verification. In fact, I check our account activity almost daily online."

Vargas said, "That's good. You can never be careful enough these days."

We'd been asking questions for ten minutes, and Hannah had barely spoken. It was time to change that. I nodded at Vargas and said, "Mrs. Booth, I'd like you to explain something to me. Forensics recovered a couple of strands of hair from Shaun Parker's body the night he was found dead." As I reached for the report Vargas had dug out of her folio, Hannah shifted her shapely legs.

I flicked the report with my fingertip and said, "This lab report conclusively identifies the hair found on Parker's body as Hannah Booth's."

Minister Booth's eyes bulged. "What? Are you certain?"

"Absolutely certain. Mrs. Booth, can you explain how that came to be?"

"I have no idea."

"You're going to have to do better than that."

Hannah crossed her arms. "I honestly don't know. Maybe he picked up a strand of my hair from working here."

Vargas said, "Were you working with Shaun Parker on the day he was found dead?"

Hannah paused and shook her head. "No, no I don't think so."

"What about the days immediately preceding his death?"

"I could have, but I don't think so."

"Did you sit in his chair, or did he sit in yours?"

"I don't know if he sat in mine, but I didn't sit in his."

"Did you ride in his vehicle?"

"No."

"Was he in your vehicle?"

"No."

I said, "Did you visit Shaun Parker's home?"

"No."

"I'm sorry for having to ask this, Minister, but Hannah, were you having an affair with Shaun Parker?"

"Are you crazy?"

Minister Booth stood up. "I'm afraid I can't allow this to go any further, Detective. If you have further questions I'm going to have to refer you to our attorney, Marcus Knight."

26

THE SHERIFF'S DOOR FINALLY OPENED, AND AFTER A STREAM of stern-faced officials came out, the door slammed shut. I hated following bad news and wished that Vargas were here. I was about to run to the bathroom when his secretary told me it was okay go in.

I rapped a knuckle on the door and entered. Chester was behind his desk, sleeves rolled up and red tie untied. Was it me, or was it stuffy in here again? I was no fan of keeping the air-conditioning low, but there'd be mold growing if he kept this up.

"Sir?"

"Take a seat, Luca."

"Sorry to hear about the Grey Oaks burglaries. Is there anything I can do to help?"

He shook his head. "You just concentrate on these killings, nothing else. You hear me? Delivering my report to the commission this morning, the only thing they asked about was this damn case. So, make sure you stay focused on it."

"Absolutely. But before we move on, I think you've got to look at these burglaries as an inside job. I mean seven houses, and I understand these guys took their time. Jacking a safe out of concrete is not a quick thing."

"Exactly how I feel. It's either the gate guards or the landscapers."

"Probably. Don't forget to look at the pest companies; they know who's around."

"They won't get far. Where're they going to fence all this high-end jewelry?"

"It'll be tough." I didn't want to depress him, so I kept quiet about a ring I'd run into in Jersey that fenced goods through an overseas network. The pundits were right for once; the world we lived in was truly global.

"I'm glad you had the sense to call. As you can imagine, Minister Booth called and then his attorney." Chester reached for a blue Post-it. "Some fellow, Marcus Knight, with a British accent. What transpired?"

"We went easy with them, trying to explore the money aspect of the case. We know they borrowed a million and that there's only two of them, the minister included, handling the church's finances. We didn't push it too hard. Without more data about their finances, it's going to be difficult to pursue that line."

"And you want me to do what?"

"Honestly, sir." I paused when I realized I used the 'H' word. "I didn't come here to ask for anything, but maybe you could ask FCU to dig into this."

Chester made a note but only said, "What about the hairs?"

"When we confronted her with the fact the hair found on Shaun Parker was hers, she claimed she didn't know how it got there. She said she wasn't with Parker on the day he was found, blah, blah, blah. The minister blew a fit when I asked if she was having an affair with Parker."

"What's your intuition telling you?"

I didn't want to tell him that lately my intuition was as reliable as a Rolex bought on the streets of Shanghai. "I'll be honest, Sheriff." Man, I must be losing it—the H word again. "Something about this Hannah Booth is off. She was weird the day we first met, and this hair on a victim is a striking piece of evidence, but it could be that she was having an affair with Parker. Other than the fact she misled us about Chapman, we don't have much to go on."

"Perhaps she was having affairs with all the victims."

It was an interesting angle, but though she had some nice lines, I couldn't imagine, or maybe I could. "That's a possibility, and one that would explain a deeper relationship to the vics above and beyond the church connection."

"She's the only one with physical evidence tying her to a body."

"We need more info, but it's slow going. The only way to speed this up would be to drag in others who work at the church and see if they'll reveal if any cheating was going on. Or we could do a physical search and see what comes up."

"A search of her house and office?"

"I think if it's an affair, we need to see if we can link her to the other victims."

"If we can limit it to a search of the church's office, and recreational, or social areas, I'll consider going to the DA. We have to respect all their religious space, or we'll be skewered in the press. If we find something on her there, we won't have to worry about blowback from the public."

It was a ballsy call. Almost too shocked to speak, I spit out, "Uhm, uh sure, no problem. A search would certainly help . . . clear things up."

"I'll have to think this over before I decide. It's a sensitive matter. Religious institutions play a huge role in the South.

The Spirit of Fellowship has a large parishioner population and does good work, I'm told."

"I understand, sir, we'd do this delicately with a small force—"

"Stop trying to convince me, Luca. I said I'd consider it. In the meantime, I expect you to keep this confidential. No one, not even your partner, should be informed about it."

27

No Maybelline girl, my ex-wife used to drive an hour to North Jersey to get her makeup. Her Swiss makeup was expensive, so going with Mary Ann to Waterside for her cosmetics was nothing.

It was another thing I liked about Mary Ann. She shopped like a man—go to a store for what you needed, buy it, and leave—no lingering around, paging through racks of clothes you didn't need nor come to buy.

After making her purchase, we grabbed seats at Brio's bar, which was hot and empty. A bank of fans played havoc with my napkin but made it comfortable. We ordered glasses of Riesling to go with Mary Ann's kale salad and my grilled mahi-mahi. After clinking glasses, I took a sip of wine. It was ice-cold and refreshing. I pecked her cheek, and we made small talk.

A bartender delivering our food interrupted my study of Mary Ann's neckline.

Swallowing my first forkful of mahi, Mary Ann pointed to a TV. "Uh-oh. Take a look at that."

Several dozen people, some with signs, were chanting in

front of The Spirit of Fellowship Church. A reporter from WINK News was speaking to Nick Santangelo. Scrolling across the TV was the closed-captioned conversation. "We believe our church and leadership are being unfairly targeted by the sheriff's department. Not one shred of evidence implicating anyone has been produced. Yet they continue to harass Minister Booth and his wife."

My fork clattered onto the bar. "Shit, it's going to be impossible now."

"What's impossible?"

I kept my eyes on the TV. "Uh, nothing. You know everything."

"Frank, what are you talking about?"

The segment was still playing. How much time were they going to give this? "Nothing. I meant, you know, investigating anyone at the church."

"Frank, you remember what we said about being truthful with each other?"

Suddenly, there was my mother, bending down with a finger in my face. "I . . . the sheriff said not to say anything to anyone."

"I certainly hope I'm not just anyone."

Man, did I want to get back to my mahi. "Of course, you're not. Look, why don't we finish dinner and talk later."

She pushed her plate away. "I'm not hungry."

Jesus Christ! Is she kidding me? "But you didn't eat anything."

"Look, if we can't trust each other, we've got nothing."

"No doubt, and I do trust you, it's just that the sheriff—"

"You mean the guy whose direct order you disobeyed? Spare me the loyalty bullshit, Frank."

She should have been a lawyer. I dragged her plate back

and said, "Okay, okay. You're right. I'll tell you, but it had nothing to do with you. I was trying to—"

"Fess up, Frank."

Lowering my voice, I told her about the possibility Chester would get us a subpoena.

"I can't imagine Chester doing that." She pointed to the TV.

"Maybe, but we've ID'd her hair, and I know the pressure is mounting on him."

"I still don't think he's gonna go for it."

I wanted to tell her she was wrong, but my night was riding on it, so I just shrugged. Wanting a happy ending to our date tonight, I told the bartender to get us each another glass of wine.

SPRAWLED out on Vargas's couch, I complained the movie playing was too predictable and grabbed the remote. Flicking through channels, a news report on WINK caught my eye. It was the story on The Spirit of Fellowship Church. I watched what was basically a repeat of what we had seen at Brio and was about to click to another channel when the newscaster began reading a statement from the sheriff's office,

"The sheriff's office denies it is targeting the church or Minister Booth and his wife. While we respect the privacy of The Spirit of Fellowship Church and the rights of all religious institutions to practice their beliefs, we are charged with protecting the safety of all Collier County citizens. If we fail to follow the evidence linking members of the church to the so-called Aquatic Assassin we'd be derelict in our duties."

I sat up. "You see, Mary Ann, I told you, he's gonna get the subpoena. Chester finally grew some balls."

"He had to issue that statement. No way he can let a protest intimidate him."

"I think it's more than that. Chester thinks Hannah is involved."

"He said that?"

"Not directly, but that was the vibe I was getting from him."

"Another hunch, Frank?"

"Just a feeling, that's all. Maybe we'll find out tomorrow."

"Put on *American Idol*. I wanna see if the girl with the tattoos made it through."

"Yeah right, you just wanna see that country hick you like, Luke Bryan."

Vargas gave me a barefoot kick as a text came in on my phone. I put *Idol* on and checked my cell. It was a text from Kayla.

"Where you going?"

"Time for a leak."

I sat on the bowl and opened the message: 'Hi Frank. I hope everything is going good for you. Sorry I haven't been in touch, but I've had a lot going on. I'll tell you when I see you. I'm coming to Naples in two weeks and would love to see you.'

My heart didn't skip a beat, but something ran up my chest. I read it again and debated deleting it.

28

PEELING OFF MY SUIT, I LAY ON THE CABANA'S BED KNOWING I had to answer Kayla's text. Well, I really didn't have to—I wanted to. It was dangerous, but Kayla was different, and we never got the chance to see what would happen. What would happen? What's wrong with you, Luca? You had two dates, that's it.

The rain began to beat on the window as I got dressed. I was supposed to meet a buddy for a burger and, without a garage, was gonna get soaked getting to my car. Down on my knees, I pulled a plastic bin from under the bed and rooted through it for my purple polo shirt. Banging my knee, I cursed the size of the cabana. How long could I stay in this shoebox?

I gotta call that Realtor and check out the place she mentioned. I didn't want to part with my savings, but what the hell? Putting it in the stock market was no sure thing.

Peering through the blinds, the rain intensified. Pulling my phone out, I tapped a text to Kayla, telling her to let me know when she was in town. Then I left a message for the Realtor to see if I could get in to see that house.

I WAS SITTING at the bar in the La Moraga when a call from Sheriff Chester came in. I threw a ten on the bar and answered the call as I headed to the door.

"This is Detective Luca."

"You got a minute, Frank?"

Pushing through the doors, I said, "Absolutely. What's up, sir?"

"Just got a call from Agent Haines, said it was a courtesy call. They're executing a search warrant on The Spirit of Fellowship Church."

"What? When?"

"They're at the church now. They went to the Middle District Federal Court in Fort Myers."

I walked into the rain and turned around. "Based on what?"

"They received a call on their hotline about a gun in Hannah Booth's office. It was anonymous; guy said he worked at the church."

"I wonder why he called the FBI instead of us? You think the Feds are being straight with us?"

"Frankly, I'm not sure at this point. At least we don't have to worry about a backlash from the public. They come up empty, and I'll make damn sure everyone knows it was the Feds who conducted it."

"They going to take this away from us?"

"I don't know. Let's see what, if anything, they find."

"I'm gonna take a run up there; see what's going on."

"No, Frank. I don't want a picture of any of us ending up in the papers. Haines said he'd call when they were done."

"I'm heading into the office."

"It's not necessary. I'll let you know when they're done."

"I'm going anyway. I won't be able to do anything else with this hanging out there."

"It's your call, Frank."

"And, sir, I appreciate the heads-up."

I put my hands over my head and ran to my car.

VARGAS HAD BROUGHT me in a sandwich, and I was wolfing it down when Chester called. Listening, I dropped the sandwich on its wrapper and hung up.

"Chester said the Feds found a gun in Hannah's office. He's on the way in. Haines is bringing the gun in."

"They're going to turn it over to us?"

"Didn't say that, but maybe they want to test it here instead of running it up to Fort Myers."

"I don't know. That doesn't make sense. They never trust the local labs, and theirs is only a half hour away."

"We have a good lab here, and Haines knows it. Who knows, maybe they're really only doing an assist here."

"I think Chester orchestrated the entire thing, Frank."

"You think so?"

"He needed cover, and using the Feds, he's got it. Don't forget, he's publicly elected."

"What do you make about the call to the tip line?"

"I don't think they'd fabricate that. It probably came in, and Haines told Chester, who suggested the Feds go in."

It made sense, but would Chester really lie to me? I tossed it around a second when what Vargas said echoed in my ear: 'he was an elected official.' Chester was a politician. Of course, he lied.

HAINES HANDED the Colt .45 to a technician. "I hope this helps you guys solve the case, Frank."

Help me? I wanted to body slam Haines.

Vargas moved between Haines and me, saying, "Let's see where this leads."

The snap the technician's glove made as he pulled it on focused me on the matters at hand. He placed the gun in a special hood and filled a container with liquid superglue. The specialist closed the door to the hood and dialed up the heat.

I took a step closer to the unit, looking for any white spots that would form from the oils left by a fingerprint. I cupped my hands around my eyes and leaned in. There didn't seem to be anything white forming.

The technician said, "It looks like it was wiped clean."

"Can you do anything more?"

"It's always tough to recover good prints from a firearm given the textured grips. You see that spot, on the right side of the barrel?"

Squinting, I saw the tiniest speck of white. "Barely."

"I'll brush it and see if it can be enhanced, but I think it's a waste of time."

Haines said, "Forget it. best you're gonna get is a partial, and a good defense attorney will tear it apart. Let's move to the ballistics."

He was right, but he wouldn't hear it from me.

The technician shut the machine down and went over the gun with a magnifier. "Nothing to work with. Let's go to the tank."

The basement had a musty smell. I got closer to Vargas, hoping her perfume would act as a counterbalance. A twenty-foot-long steel tank, shining under the fluorescent lighting, was the only thing in the room. The hood of the three-foot-wide vessel was up and the water inside clear.

There were only two pairs of earmuffs on the wall, and I grabbed a pair, followed by the tech. Haines said, "We'll wait outside."

When the steel door slammed behind Vargas and Haines, the technician put the barrel of the gun into an angled shaft.

A splash of water rose as the gun cracked. The tech retrieved the bullet with a basket, and after hanging our ear protection back on the wall, we left.

VARGAS PULLED me back and whispered, "I don't know why we're wasting time watching all this. We should be preparing arrest documents."

"What are you talking about? We can't let him hijack this."

"He said he was taking a back seat."

"Yeah, and you believe him?"

"That's what he told me."

"Yeah, what else did he tell you?"

"Nothing."

"I saw the way he was looking at you."

"What are you talking about, Frank?"

"Forget it, okay? just forget it."

"You wanna waste your time—go for it. I'm going back to the office."

She was starting to piss me off. I was looking forward to Kayla coming into town. Shake things up. I didn't need this bullshit.

I WASN'T in the laboratory when the doctors were looking at the slides of my cancer, but I couldn't imagine them putting in more effort than this guy was. He was moving between two large microscopes and a tablet that he tapped notes into.

My ass was killing me from the stainless-steel stool, and it was cold in here. The only good thing was Haines had given up on me and went to get a bite to eat.

Finally, the tech pushed his stool back and got up, nodding. "No doubt it's a match. These bullets came from the same gun."

"Are you sure there's enough consecutive matches?"

"I said, no doubt."

"Humor me, will you? This is a big case. What makes you so sure?"

"First off, there's the left-hand twist which only Colts have. And there are enough striations that line up. They're clean, and there is a minimum of six sets of consecutive matches."

That was more than enough to withstand an attack by F. Lee Bailey. "How quick can we get a report?"

"I can get a preliminary to you in an hour. But the full one is not going to be until, say, noon tomorrow."

"Thanks. Email it to me as soon as the prelim is ready."

It was damn near midnight when I sent a text to Vargas that the gun was a match.

29

We sat around the fake stone table in Chester's office. The sheriff, in jeans and a red polo shirt, looked fresher than any of us. Haines, white sleeves rolled up and clothes wrinkled, hadn't said much before DA Thume arrived.

With the district attorney seated between Chester and me, Haines began pushing for an arrest of Hannah Booth, claiming the evidence provided solid ground to charge her in the death of Joseph Chapman.

DA Thume asked, "Are you considering filing federal charges?"

"No, no. This is the sheriff's case. We're only offering assistance."

The DA said, "We have enough to press charges in the Chapman murder, but I'll leave the decision to proceed to the sheriff."

Chester looked at me. "What do you think?"

"I don't believe arresting her is the way to play this. We've got four homicides to solve, and at this point only a connection on one of them to Hannah. We need more. We should talk to her before making an arrest."

Haines said, "You're not going to get anything more out of her by not filing charges. Either way, she's going to have representation."

"Maybe, maybe not."

"Did you forget we conducted a search? They're going to be defensive."

What a revelation. Talking to the law makes everyone defensive. "With the press coverage of the search, maybe a tip will come in. It's possible she's being framed."

Haines stifled a chuckle. "I'm sure she'll say that. Why not arrest her; pressure her; see if she cracks? If she's not guilty it'll come out eventually."

An image of the Barrow kid swinging from his cell sent a shudder through me, prompting Thume to say, "It is cold in here."

I said, "Sir, I don't have to remind everyone about how this will look if the minister's wife is arrested, and there's insufficient evidence."

Haines said, "Hold on. We're totally within protocol. The murder weapon was found in her office and her hair on a victim's body."

Looking at the sheriff, I said, "If it's really our case to handle, my call is to hold off. Let me interview her."

The sheriff said, "Look, it's late. I really appreciate everyone's input and dedication. Hannah's under surveillance. Nothing's going to change overnight. I say we sleep on it, wait till morning before deciding how to proceed."

VARGAS SAID she'd be in later; her stomach was still bothering her. Of all the days she had to be sick. I needed to talk things through, now I'd have to figure this out on my own. Grabbing my coffee and bagel, I stepped into the humidity, hoping she'd make it in before noon.

Balancing my coffee, I unlocked the door to our office when my name was called.

"Luca, got a strange call last night on the Aquatic case."

"Strange? I don't like the way that sounds, Tommy."

"A guy called last night claiming that Hannah had been having an affair with both Chapman and Cornwall."

"Shit!" Hot coffee spilled on my hand.

"Got the shakes?"

"Yeah, right. Tell me about the call."

"About eleven fifteen this guy calls in. Montgomery said he sounded like he had a cloth over the mouthpiece. He said the minister's wife was having sex with two of the guys who got killed, Joe Chapman and Dick Cornwall."

"Anonymous?"

"Yep."

"Montgomery have any idea of the age of the caller?"

"Best guess was twenty-five to fifty."

"Tell him thanks for narrowing it down for me. Anything else?"

"Nada."

The chessboard just got jostled. I needed a sounding board.

"Vargas, how you feeling?"

She said, "Pretty much the same. I don't know if I'm gonna make it in."

"Maybe you should go to the doctor, then."

"I'll see if it gets better today."

"Don't wait till it's too late, like me. It could be—"

"What, do you think it's something serious, like cancer?"

"No, no. Nothing like that. Just go to the doctor, will you?"

"It'll probably pass. What's going on with the case? Did Chester make a decision yet?"

"No, and it's just gotten more complicated. After the search, a call came in to the tip line last night. This guy tells Montgomery that Hannah was having affairs with both Chapman and Cornwall."

"Oh my God."

"It's nuts. I don't know if I buy it, but if it's true, a whole world of possibilities opens up."

"You don't think Minister Booth found out and—"

Damn, that never entered my mind. "Don't think so, but can't rule it out. More likely, she was playing around with not only these two but others and somebody got jealous."

"I don't know; more likely, Hannah killed them to prevent the affairs from becoming public."

"I know women, and I don't believe it."

"Oh, so you know women?"

"You know what I mean."

"No, I don't. Why don't you tell me?"

"Come on, I'm just saying that something's telling me it wasn't her."

"Since you know so much about women, you must be right, then."

"Can we not do this? Can we talk about the case?"

"We need to check out the call. See if there is anything to Hannah being unfaithful. She may say something if we can promise confidentiality."

"You want to ask her about it?"

"I know you think you know women, but I'm a woman,

and we girls tell each other things we'd never tell a man. I gotta run to the bathroom."

I said a little something to make a point, and Mary Ann goes and makes a big, damn thing about it. What's up with that? Geez, maybe she was getting too comfortable with me. If this was how it was going to be, I didn't know if it was for me.

Was she gonna make it in today? Maybe it was her stomach making her bitchy. When I wasn't feeling good I probably wasn't fun to be around either. My desk phone rang.

"Frank, I've decided to hold off on arresting Hannah Booth. I'll give you more time to build a stronger case against her. We've got to be certain on this one."

Just this one? If she wasn't the wife of a minister she'd be in the can now. "I think it's the right call, Sheriff. We have a couple of pieces of information that just came in and need vetting."

"Good. Keep me apprised."

I grabbed my jacket off the back of my chair. "Sure thing."

"I'm counting on you, Frank. I don't have to tell you the pressure this office is under."

"Don't worry, sir. I've got it."

Stopped at a light at Livingston Road I called Mary Ann again to see how she was feeling. She was still sick and promised to see a doctor. I told her that Chester was holding off on the arrest and that I was on my way to see Hannah.

30

"He's Got the Whole World in His Hands" was playing in the all-purpose room, where a half a dozen people, including Minister Booth, were working. People were taking cans of food out of large laundry carts and bagging them. Minister Booth was carrying a loaded bag to a table covered with brown bags when I caught his eye. He pulled his lips in, set the load down and headed toward me.

"Hello, Detective Luca." He extended a hand. "It's nice to see you, but I believe I made it clear that future conversations go through our attorney, Marcus Knight."

I shook his hand. "I understand, but if you would give me a minute, I can explain."

"That was a very unpleasant episode last night. The congregation is upset."

"It wasn't us. That was the FBI, and they never consulted with us."

"Really? Are you saying you had no prior knowledge about the warrant?"

"None whatsoever."

"I'll accept that at face value."

"Thank you. It's true."

Booth looked over his shoulder and said, "As you can see, we're busy. Quite a few parishioners are staying away, given the controversy, so I've got to get help, even more than usual. What is on your mind?"

"I hope you can hear me out."

"Go ahead, Detective."

"As the search last night proved, your wife is a suspect, and now, finding the gun makes her a stronger suspect. Frankly, the only one. I'll admit I had my suspicions about her, but I no longer think she had anything to do with it."

"And what caused this change of heart?"

"This may sound strange to you, Minister, but first and foremost—my instinct. Something isn't right, and I have ideas about what that is, but it's early."

"That's not strange to a man of God. Many of our feelings are actually communications from God. People call them by other names, like your conscious speaking or coincidences, but it's God. What else were you going to say?"

"There's been a couple of pieces of new information."

"That'll clear up the confusion about Hannah?"

"I hope so. But I'd like to speak with her, alone."

"She won't agree to talk without me present."

"You can convince Hannah that it's in her best interests to talk with me. It really is, Minister. There are no games being played here."

"I'm a man of God and a man of my word. I'll assume you're also a man who keeps his word."

FRAMED BY CROSS-SHAPED EARRINGS, Hannah Booth's face had a sour look.

"I don't know why we agreed to this, especially after last night."

"We had nothing to do with that."

She rolled her blue eyes, which didn't appear as stunning as usual. Maybe the spinster bun her blond hair was pulled into had dimmed them.

"It's true. It was the FBI."

"Whatever."

I wondered if lying to a minister's wife made the sin of lying worse. "In spite of what you may believe, I never considered you a viable suspect."

Hannah grunted as she shifted in her seat but said nothing more.

"Look, we may have gotten off on the wrong foot, but I'm here to help you."

Another silent, though shorter, eye roll.

"I'm gonna be straight with you, and you need to be straight with me, or I can't help you. You got that?"

She shrugged and looked at her nails. I wanted to choke the bitch.

"Last night, a tip came in to the hotline." I studied her closely. "The caller claimed that you had affairs with Joseph Chapman and Dick Cornwall."

She blinked and shook her head. "That's ridiculous."

"Is it?"

"Of course, it is. I never had an affair with either of them, or anyone, for that matter. It's against God's word. A violation of his commandments."

"Did you ever flirt with either of them?"

"What kind of woman do you think I am, Detective? The

book of Exodus, chapter twenty, 'Thou shalt not covet thy neighbor's wife.'" Hannah leaned forward. "I don't conduct myself in a flirtatious manner. And for the record, I love my husband."

On a scale of one to ten, the denial was close to a ten, but I'd seen guys with pants around their ankles deny they cheated on their wives. She threw that Bible verse as if it were an independent confirmation.

"Mrs. Booth, I'm a homicide detective. I've seen it all, and I don't care what people do, so long as they aren't creating corpses. I just want to help you and solve this case, so I'll ask you again. Did you ever have an affair or sexual relations of any kind, even Bill Clinton's type, with either Chapman or Cornwall?"

"It sounds like you're saying that admitting to an affair would help clear my name. Well, if it would, I couldn't admit to something I never did."

Okay, her denial was a ten. "Understood. Now, about the gun, the Colt .45 seized from this office last night. Was that your gun?"

She arched her back, "No. I've never owned a gun or even shot one."

Interesting. People who shoot usually say fired a gun, not shot a gun. "Never? Not at a gun range, as a kid? Some uncle, letting you get a thrill?"

"Never. Weapons kill. The world would be a better place if we didn't have guns."

I wanted to ask her why God didn't interfere, preventing humans from inventing firearms, but I had an interview to conduct. I asked, "Do you have any idea how this gun ended up in your office?"

"I don't know. I was shocked last night. I still can't believe it."

"Any possibilities you can think of?"

"Only one that makes sense—for some reason, I'm being framed."

"It's a possibility. Who do you think could be behind something like that?"

"I don't know. Someone is trying to ruin my reputation."

"Do you or your husband have any enemies?"

"No, no. Gabriel is the kind of man you could never dislike."

She was right. If he told someone to go to hell, they'd ask him for directions.

"I know it's a sore subject, but could it be something to do with a disagreement in the way the church was run?"

She shook her head. "I can't imagine that a disagreement over our mission could lead to something like this. That would be crazy."

She needed more exposure to the human condition. "People can get passionate, lose control, and rationalize the strangest things."

"I guess anything is possible, but I haven't a clue who it could be."

"Think further back. Is there something that happened, or someone you had an argument with—anything like that? People have held on to slights, perceived or real, for decades before taking action. Is there anyone you can think of?"

She leaned a cheek on a palm. "Nothing comes to mind. I've been through some very difficult times in my life. My son; he was hooked on drugs and died from an overdose." She took a sharp breath through her nose. "People made all kinds of accusations that amounted to slander. At the time, I thought I'd never recover, but through God's grace I did. Now, I've got to get through this."

"It must have been rough. I'm sorry for your loss."

She bit her lip and whispered, "It was devastating. It still is. I think of him every single day."

Emotion was good in an interview but not the direction this was going. I cleared my throat.

"It could be someone from the past who has it in for you. It may have nothing to do with your son. Why don't you think some more about this, and let me know if you recall anything?"

She nodded. "Okay."

"Now, the church recently took a large loan out—a million dollars." I let it hang for a second. "Could something be going on? Maybe a theft or embezzlement of some kind?"

"We took the loan out to expand our mission and outreach. There were a few, myself included, who disagreed over it, but Minister Booth has the final say and went ahead with it."

"Why were you opposed to borrowing the money?"

"I felt we were adding too much risk, and by expanding we could be stretching ourselves too thin. My husband works nonstop, and we barely have time together."

"He does seem committed. More like he's married to the church, right?"

She nodded silently.

"You're home alone a lot, then."

"Most nights, but Sundays, after services, we're always home together."

"That's a lot of time alone."

"We work together. It's not like I don't see him."

I lowered my voice. "Hannah, you got to be completely honest with me. I don't care what anyone's marriage is like. Lord knows, mine was no picnic, and it was my fault. You can count on me to keep it quiet, but I need to know if you had any involvement, other than work, with Chapman or Cornwall."

Her believability sank as she hesitated, meekly saying, "I didn't do it."

31

———

IT WAS HOT. I KICKED MY FEET OUT FROM UNDER THE SHEET, sending a flash of pain to my lower back. *Who will go for us?* kept looping in my mind. I couldn't fall back asleep. Every time I checked the clock, its red numbers only advanced a couple of minutes.

Closing my eyes, I couldn't shake the voice. I knew it wasn't a dream; it was God speaking. He knew I was afraid and had stopped doing his work. The police were putting a lot of resources into finding me, and I had to keep a low profile to avoid being taken off the battlefield.

His words were crystal clear: "Who shall I send? Who will go for us?" I replayed his call for help over and over. It was dangerous work, but the rewards eternal. In Romans 2, verses 6-7, it said, 'God renders to every man according to his deeds. Those who persevere and do his work, receive honor and eternal life.'

How could I say no? Who would ever say no? I threw the covers off, and before my feet hit the tile I said, "Here am I, Lord. Send me." There was evil to stamp out, and I was going to resume the battle, starting with one of the wickedest serpents to slither on God's earth.

I'd been careful to avoid evening the score. I knew I couldn't hide my motivations from God. He knew everything, so I waited, disposing of other sinful, immoral felons before going after this depraved punk, Bobby.

Piece of shit was no better than his evil father, Paul. What a farce, Paul, the devil incarnate, was named after an apostle. The bastard was gifted with at least three so-called second chances. If Paul would've remained behind bars as he should have, my mom would be alive.

My head began pounding, and my vision blurred. I extended my arm and felt my way to the bathroom. I kept the light off and grabbed my meds. Twisting the top off, I stuck a finger in, rolled three pills up, and hit the faucet to wash them down. Gently lowering myself onto the toilet, I waited for the razor-sharp pain to ease. As the pain ebbed, the memory of my mother's death seeped in.

On that day she was late coming home, which happened from time to time when the grocery store was busy toward the end of her shift. But an hour later it felt different. I went outside and sat on the front steps to wait.

Dusk turned to night, and I was crying when my next-door neighbor, Mrs. Hawley, came home. She took me in, heated up a bowl of soup and made some calls. Slurping soup, I heard her say, "She's missing. She left work two hours ago." Mrs. Hawley put a hand on her hip. "No, she wouldn't. Her eight-year-old kid is home alone, sitting on the steps waiting for her."

I listened, my concern elevating when she said, "I'm telling you, something's happened to her. She's a responsible woman. I don't care about any of your protocol. You've got to do something."

When Mr. Hawley came home, we went to the police station. It was scary. The policemen were real nice to me, but they said I had to stay and wait for a lady to get me. I sat on a wooden bench as Mr. Hawley told me everything would be all right. As he disappeared down a corridor, I began crying. No one was helping to find my mother.

It felt like a long time until a lady came and sat next to me. She smelled like an orange and had clogs on with a long skirt. I had to go with her until my mom came home, she said. It was the law and that there was nothing to be afraid of. Her mouth was moving but I couldn't hear anything she said. Then I remember she placed my hand in her sweaty hand and led me to a van.

There was another kid in the van who was younger and sobbing badly. I broke down and started calling for my mom as we rolled away. They took us to a place that looked like a school but had bars on the windows. There was a smell, I later realized was bleach, that I can still feel in the back of my throat almost thirty years later. They told me I'd see my mother in the morning, but I knew I'd never see her again.

After being forced to shower with a soap that smelled like spoiled milk, they gave me itchy pajamas and brought me to a room with two rows of beds. I curled up on a hard mattress, staring at the wall until I fell asleep.

In the morning, I said I didn't deserve to be in jail and that I wanted to go home, but they told me to be quiet and follow the rules. It was right after I threw up my lunch that I was taken to an office. I was afraid, telling them I was sorry for throwing up, but I couldn't help it. It wasn't my fault.

A bald man, wearing John Lennon glasses, was sitting behind a desk. His Adam's apple bobbed before he said, "I have some difficult news about your mother. She was killed by a very bad man."

That very bad man was Paul Hagan. I was counting on what his son Bobby said about the two of them being close, even though Paul was behind bars. It wasn't until I was twenty-five that I learned the details of what happened to my mother. Tied up like an animal in the basement of an abandoned house, she was violently raped by Hagan. While she was still alive this monster disfigured her genitals. The ghastly news made me physically ill for weeks, and when I learned Hagan had been released from prison only three weeks earlier, I fell into a depression that lasted for two years.

His son Bobby, another irredeemable bastard, was going to pay the price, and I was hoping his father would suffer as I had.

Idiots who think evil can be reformed don't get it. These people are in the devil's camp. This is war; they must be slayed.

32

———

Fifteen minutes into his daily swim, Jay McDaniel found his rhythm. He took four long strokes with his head down and turning his head left, took a deep breath. He repeated the routine, making his way from Pelican Bay's South Beach toward Clam Pass.

McDaniel was considering where to take his new girl-friend to lunch when his hand bumped into something. Concerned the wakeboard he towed along in case of an emergency had come untethered, he popped his head up.

Heart racing, McDaniel pushed his goggles up and gasped. It was a body. McDaniel shoved the body away and grabbed his board. He shouted toward the shoreline, but the beach walkers kept parading.

McDaniel positioned the wakeboard under his chest and paddled for the beach.

———

I always liked the setup at Pelican Bay. The community had a combination of beachfront high-rises and twenty different communities stretched along the shore from Vanderbilt Beach Road to Pine Ridge. There were price points from four hundred thousand to ten million, but all of them carried a premium attributed to their location and beach access.

Most of their homes weren't by the beach. There was a wide bay separating most homes from the sand, but Pelican Bay ran continuous golf cart shuttles, ferrying its residents to its north and south beaches. Each beach had restaurant facilities with amazing views. Mary Ann had a friend who lived there, and we had dinner with them twice.

The click-clacking sound our cart made slowed as we came to the end of the mile-long boardwalk. The cart deposited us by a stairway where yellow police tape sliced the stairs in half. Descending the steps, I wondered whether this was a blameless drowning or part of the killing spree that threatened my career.

The Gulf shimmered in the morning sun without the glare. Groups of beachgoers and busybodies were clustered near a line of tape that ran from the mangroves to a stake at the water's edge.

I showed my credentials to the officer acting as the gatekeeper.

"Detective, the man who found the body is over there."

He pointed to a covered deck where morning yoga classes and evening music shows were held. A pair of officers were talking to a fit, sixty-something man in a bathing suit.

"Thanks. Maybe later."

I wanted to see the body first. I couldn't imagine the towel-draped swimmer could tell me anything helpful. I ducked under the tape, realizing this was the first time I was working on the beach.

When I'd first gotten down here, I had a trace of envy for

the officers who patrolled the beach. Riding up and down the beach on an ATV was not only an easy gig, but it seemed like a crafty way to meet women.

Realizing that each step I took in the sand could bring me closer to losing my career, I paused, covering my concerns with a slow scan of the area. Inhaling deeply, I headed toward the body.

An officer on an ATV parked to shield the body got off his machine. My heart sank when I saw the corpse was a thirty-something-year-old male.

"Hiya doing, Luca."

"All good." I couldn't remember this guy's name. His tag said Brewster, but his first name wasn't even close to the tip of my tongue. I knelt by the body, swallowing the bile that ran up my throat. There were two bullet wounds in the chest.

The head was lolled back, and the mouth formed a perfect O. Was that a look of surprise?

"What's the time line here?"

"I was down by the Ritz when the call came in around eight twenty a.m. I called for a boat to grab the body, but by the time I got here fifteen minutes later, the body was on the beach."

"Who retrieved the body?"

"The guy who found the body is up at the club. This guy goes out every morning, and he ran into it swimming. He hightailed it back to shore, and a couple of the beach kids from the club went out with their boards and dragged the body in."

"You got gloves?"

"Yeah." He lifted the ATV's seat and grabbed gloves from the compartment.

"Roll him over a little. I want to check his back pockets."

The only thing in his pockets were grains of sand—no wallet, no phone, no nothing. I was trying to convince myself that this difference would be enough to cast doubt it was the same killer.

"Crazy, huh? Out swimming and run into a corpse—that'd freak out anyone."

Studying the redheaded body, I tried to envision whether this was another thug whose criminal hourglass had run out. Jeans and a tee shirt seemed to be their dress code. This stiff was solidly built, but not strong enough to repel a bullet.

The killer was winning; the evidence lay at my feet. I'd have to change tactics completely to catch him or her, that is if Chester didn't pull it from me. Taking my phone out to check when the coroner was coming, I saw another text from Kayla. Cupping my hand to block the sun, I read it:

"Hey Frank. Hope everything is all right. Maybe you missed my text, but I'll be in town next week."

<hr>

ENTERING MY OFFICE WAVING A REPORT, I said, "We got a ballistics match with Parker."

Vargas said, "And we got a name for victim five. Bobby Hagan, thirty-five years old and another habitual offender. Lived in Golden Gate."

"We've either got two killers, or someone looking to throw us off."

"Also, hate to tell you, but Chester decided against a search."

"What? Why?"

"Probably the pressure. You see the *Daily News*?"

Vargas held the paper up. A picture on the front page of

the protest sat under a headline: "Religious Freedom Under Attack?"

"What total bullshit! No wonder nobody trusts the media."

"They put the sheriff's statement at the end of the article, on page nine."

"I still can't believe he backed off. Something isn't right. We've got solid evidence. He has to follow it."

"Maybe he'll wait till things die down."

"What? Wait until we find another body floating somewhere?"

"Sit down, Frank. Let's focus on this guy Hagan."

Vargas had put together a file with Hagan's rap sheet and family contacts. His mother lived in Estero and had been notified of her son's demise. She was the natural place to start.

TAHITI MOBILE VILLAGE was just past Koreshan Park off of Broadway. The collection of trailer homes wouldn't inspire anyone to visit Tahiti, and I'd bet the Tahitian Tourist Commission would object if they knew this place existed.

Lynn Hagan lived in a pink trailer on Polynesian Loop. As far as I knew, there weren't any flamingos in Tahiti, but there were half a dozen flamingos peppering her entrance area. Vargas led the way, climbing three steps to knock on a glass-louvered door.

A pair of glasses were dangling around her sixty-something year-old neck. With lipstick three shades too red, Lynn Hagan looked like someone who worked in a Jersey diner. Vargas told her why we were here, and she stepped to the side.

Before I got to the top step I could smell cigarette smoke.

I turned my head, took a gulp of fresh air, and stepped into the mobile home. It was bigger than I expected. A worn leather couch anchored the living space, and an oak table with four chairs filled the dining area.

"Mrs. Hagan, we'd like to extend our condolences for your loss." Vargas winced and rubbed her abdomen.

Hagan reached for a pack of Lucky Strikes. "I lost Bobby a long time ago." She took a cigarette out, stuck it in her mouth, and lit it with a blue lighter.

"Can you tell us anything that would help make sense of who did this to your son?"

The tip of her cigarette turned bright orange. Exhaling, she said, "It started early, it did. Bobby had problems with his eyes, something called Uveal Coloboma. Kid had to wear these special glasses. I felt bad for him. He got teased to no end about it. Couldn't play sports and such. His father, the no-good bastard he was, tried to toughen him up—went too goddamn far, is what he did."

"We're aware of your son's trouble with the law."

She laughed. "Nice way of putting it, but his father turned him into a delinquent before he could drive. And when the no-good bastard got sent away for good, Bobby got worse— kept getting arrested. I thought moving would help, and when I heard about a church that helped people like him, we came down. I tried, but . . ." Her voice trailed off, and she took a draw on her smoke.

"Was that The Spirit of Fellowship Church?"

I moved away from the smoke she blew my way as she nodded.

I said, "What about his friends? Is there anyone you know that was close to him, that we should speak to?"

She shook her head. "We didn't see each other much. Last time I seen him was like a year ago, maybe more."

"You can't think of anyone?"

She shook her head.

As soon as we got outside, I said, "What's the matter? Your stomach bothering you again?"

"No, my side. Maybe it's the kidney."

33

THE RAINY SEASON WAS DUMPING THE LAST OF ITS DELUGE, slowing traffic to a crawl on Airport Polling Road. Worried about Mary Ann, I cut down Orange Blossom and made a right onto Goodlette Frank and headed to NCH. The weather and traffic mirrored my day; it started out sunny, then body number five showed up, and everything went to shit.

Traffic was backed up at the Immokalee intersection, and trying to see around a pickup truck, I saw it: a Honda Accord with one of its backup lights on while it was stopped at a traffic light. The same car that Kelp, who lived in Aqua, mentioned.

Inching to the car in front of me, I tried to recall if Kelp mentioned what side of the car had a backup light on. This one was on the left. The light changed, and the clown in front of me was looking at his damn phone. The Honda was out of sight when we finally started moving. I put my strobes on and hit the siren.

Cars parted. I snaked through, getting behind the Honda, which slowed and pulled over. Yanking the steering wheel, I passed the Accord, realizing it wasn't a backup light but a reflection. Approaching Airport Polling, I shut the siren and lights and made a U-turn.

There were ten people on the line for visitors. I flashed my badge and went around the barrier. I get the attempt at hospital security, but having some volunteer ask to see your driver's license before admitting you is zero security.

Mary Ann stirred, smiling when I entered her room. She looked pale and small in the bed. There was an IV in her arm, leading to a clear bag on a pole.

"Nice. You're lying here resting and leaving it to me to bag all the bad guys?"

She propped herself up. "Hi Frank. It's so good to see you."

I kissed her cheek. "How you feeling?"

"Pretty good. I haven't had to ask for painkillers in a while."

"What's the doctor saying?"

"Ruled out an infection. Going to do some tests tomorrow. I'm hoping to avoid a colonoscopy."

"If you gotta have one, it's no big deal. As long as they find out what's going on."

"I'll probably get out tomorrow. One of the doctors said he thought it might be something to do with my ovaries."

"A cyst or something?"

"Maybe. How you doing, now that we've got a fifth body?"

"Haines is still pushing for an arrest."

"Yeah, I know. He told me."

"He called you?"

"No, he came by this morning."

I looked around the room for flowers. "Why'd he come here?"

"To see how I was. He was concerned about me."

"I'll bet he was. I don't trust that guy."

"You don't seem to trust any men, Frank."

Was she right? "That's not true. I just don't want him around you. He's trying to weasel his way to taking the case from us. He thinks it's Hannah, and now, with the new body, is ramping the pressure up."

"That's ridiculous. He said it was our case, and it is. He hasn't done anything to prove he wasn't sincere about it."

Sincere? Why'd she use that word? "If he succeeds in convincing everyone to arrest Hannah, it'll screw up our chances to solve this."

"You really don't think she did it? That's quite a reversal, Frank."

"She's off, weird, but you know, she lost a kid, and that's something you never come all the way back from."

"That's the most sensible thing you said since hello."

Sometimes she really got on my nerves. "Ha-ha. I don't think she did it, and if Haines stays out of this, we'll get the real bastard who's doing this."

"I hope you're right, Frank. But Hannah Booth is all we got at this point."

"We're still running down all the Honda Accords. Maybe we'll finally get a damn break."

My phone vibrated. "It's Chester. Damn, he's probably going to move on Hannah."

I gave a thumbs-up to Mary Ann as Chester talked, and when I hung up I pumped a fist in the air. "Yes!"

"What happened?"

"Guess who was sitting in a Lee County cell last night? Hannah Booth."

"What happened?"

"She was picked up on a DUI around seven last night and did a dry out overnight."

"Oh my God."

"Chester got a call from their attorney, that Knight guy, claiming it absolved his client of the killings."

"Do we have a time of death on Hagan yet?"

"Nothing firm, but looks like around eight o'clock last night. No way it could be Hannah."

34

ONE OF THE LAST PLACES ON EARTH WITHOUT A CCTV WAS my office, and boy was I regretting it when Haines walked in.

"Hey, Frank, just wanted to admit I was wrong, dead wrong, about Hannah Booth."

All I could muster was, "It happens."

He put two hands on the back of the chair in front of my desk. "I feel terrible. I really do. I wasted a lot of your time."

"Looks like she's being framed."

"You think it might be her husband, the minister?"

"I'd have to hand in my badge if it turns out to be him. He'd have to be a better actor than Nicholson to pull this off."

"I wish I could make this up, somehow. I'll stay out of your way, but if you need anything, the FBI has unlimited resources, and they're all yours—just ask."

"Thanks. I appreciate it."

"Well, I'll leave you to it, then. Good luck."

"Thanks."

Haines was half out the door when I said, "Hold up a sec. It's a long shot, but I'm following a lead on a car that may have been seen at one or two of the crime scenes. As luck would have it, it might be a Honda Accord. There's like twenty thousand of them in the damn county. We're running them down as fast as we can, but is there anything you think you can do?"

"Hm, maybe we can run a cross-check of the owners, and get their cell phones. Then we could get the phone companies to give us the location data and cross-reference to the crime scenes."

"You can do that?"

Haines smiled. "Officially, we can't, but let me see what I can do. I may have to fib to get what you need. I'm hoping we can keep this between us?"

Haines was putting his neck on the line for me? "Of course."

"I thought so. What list you working with?"

I told him we had cross-checked for anyone with a record and shared what we had on Honda Accords registered in Collier.

Haines said, "To save some time, you mind if I operate from Mary Ann's desk for a second?"

I did. "Sure, you can use her desk."

"Okay, email me that list."

I sent the list and pretended to be working as Haines cajoled someone to cross-reference the motor vehicle database with cell phone ownership.

"I'm gonna run up to Fort Myers. He said to give them a couple of hours."

IT WAS JUST BEFORE five when Haines called.

"Check your inbox, Frank. I just forwarded a cross-ref

list."

I scanned the first two columns of an Excel spreadsheet. One had a list of Accord owners, and in a second column were cell numbers for most of them. Then there were another five columns for each of the crime scenes that were either blank or marked with an X.

"I gotta say, that's impressive, Tom. I guess nothing is really private anymore."

"And it's getting worse. We've got tools being developed that'll put the colonoscopy doctors out of business."

I laughed. "That's funny, man."

"Unfortunately, it's just about true. We've got so much data it's a struggle to manage it."

I wanted to ask him if he could tell me which cars' backup lights were malfunctioning, but I had to hold some information back. "I can imagine."

"So, this list, you'll notice there's about twenty-five without cell numbers attached, and the important thing to remember is the locations are affected by, one, if they have their phone on, and two, what cell tower they ping off of. Plus, nothing is stopping the killer from having his phone some nights and not others. If he or she is as smart as we think they are, they probably would turn their phone off to confuse things. Or they could have simply used another car."

I was sure Haines heard my crest falling. Then I remembered that everybody eventually makes mistakes. "This is helpful, man. I really appreciate it."

"Anytime. You need something, all you got to do is ask."

Sorting the list, I came up with fourteen cars with an X in four of the five boxes and another twenty-nine that had three of five. I ran the forty-eight names through the DMV interface, eliminating nine who were over seventy-five years old.

The room darkened as I scrolled through the thirty-nine

names left. I knew the focus had to be on the first fourteen when an idea stuck me. A crack of thunder sounded as I picked up the phone.

"Tom, it's Frank Luca."

"That was fast. What's up?"

"Is there a way you guys can see if anyone on this list owns a boat?"

"That's not a bad idea, but there's no evidence the killer used a boat."

"Maybe, but don't forget about the body that swimmer ran into. I gotta feeling about this."

"All right then, I'm sure there's a database we can tap into, and as long as the boat's registered, we'll find it."

"Thanks again, Tom."

"Anytime."

I READ the bulletin the sheriff issued, asking all patrol cars to be on the lookout for vehicles whose backup lights were on while the car was moving forward. Swiveling my chair, I studied the map on the wall behind me. Five red pins marked the spots where the bodies were found. Each location was fairly remote, excepting the one by Palm River, which I thought had floated west anyway.

My eyes kept drifting toward the section of the map showing the Gordon River. The area, just west of Naples Airport, was the perfect place to dump a body. It was relatively undeveloped, and at night, virtually deserted. Why hadn't the killer used this spot yet? Was it being saved? Or did they live nearby?

Mapping the addresses left me with four who lived within a mile of the river. One, essentially on the river's bank. Instead of letting a patrol car commandeer my hunch, I jotted down the address and headed into the rain.

35

———————

PULLING OFF GOODLETTE INTO MANGROVE BAY, MY expectations tumbled. Ethan Dwyer lived in a new community featuring tightly spaced, white clapboard homes in a Key West style. Knowing the architecturally detailed homes were selling for over two million dollars almost made me turn around. But I reminded myself that you never really knew anybody.

A couple of amber lights shone through the windows, but there was no movement. I wondered if the Honda Accord was sitting behind the brown, two-car garage door. After patting my holster, I flipped up my collar and trotted to the front door.

There was a nice overhang protecting the front door, which had a glazed window. Looking for movement in the window, I rang the bell. Nothing. I edged closer to the door and rang it again. It sounded, but no one answered. I trotted back to the car.

I hated using an umbrella. Running in and out of the car you'd get a little wet without one, but using one you got wet opening and closing it. And the stupid thing would drip water everywhere when you were done.

Circling through the small neighborhood, I parked diagonally across from Dwyer's house. While staring at the house, I debated whether to try the next closest house on the list when a car turned into the neighborhood. I slinked down. It looked like a Honda, but the Civic model. It slowed as it passed Dwyer's house, and there seemed to be a male at the wheel.

Ducking as the car passed me, I sprang up hoping to see a malfunctioning backup light. Nothing but a disability license plate. I jotted the plate number down. A minute later, the car came back out and turned onto Goodlette. After calling the plate in, they verified the owner had a prosthetic leg. A one-legged, busybody out in the pouring rain?

My eyes were bleary, and the whoosh of the wipers were lulling me to sleep. Needing coffee, I drove to the Starbucks next to Rosedale Pizza. I was going to do the drive-through but decided instead that getting a little wet was worth the price for an order of garlic twists.

I dashed through the rain and yanked Rosedale's door open, rewarded by the comforting smell of pizza and garlic. After debating whether to get a small pie, I ordered a bag of twists to go and ran next door for a cup of coffee as they made the twists.

Looking at the intersection of Pine Ridge and Goodlette as my coffee was being made, I saw a Honda Accord whose backup light on the right side was on. Eyes fixed on the Accord, I bolted out the door. The barista yelled as I splashed my way to the car.

Throwing the siren on, I ripped my way out of the lot. The Honda had made a right onto Goodlette. I sped after it as the rain intensified. Approaching Vanderbilt Beach Road, the

Accord was in the middle of the intersection. The light turned yellow and I floored the gas.

Red lights suddenly brightened in the car in front of me. Swerving left around the slowing car, I noticed a black pickup truck jumping the light. Yanking the wheel to my right, my car began to spin, hydroplaning toward a light pole.

I got a mouthful of airbag, my neck snapping back as my car tilted on two wheels. When it bounced back on the ground, I was staring at the front end of the pickup truck as we skidded to a stop.

The only sound I heard was the wipers beating back and forth. Wincing, I reached for the radio, issuing an all-points bulletin for the Accord. I moved each limb slowly. Other than a soreness on the outside of a knee and a surging headache, I was fine.

Over oncoming siren sounds, a guy with a goatee opened the driver's door and asked if I was okay. He helped unbuckle my belt. I tried to avoid going to the hospital, but seeing the state of my car and knowing protocol I quickly surrendered.

The hospital wasted three hours of my time to tell me something I already knew—nothing was broken. The doctor suggested I wear a neck brace to help with the whiplash.

Chester sent a patrolman named Esposito to pick me up. He parked under the portico shaped like a bunny slope. I got in, ripping the brace off my neck. Tapping my cell phone, I said, "I heard you got the Accord."

"Yep."

Haines answered my call. "Tom, it's Frank. Yeah, I'm okay, just a little banged up. Look, I need a favor, okay?"

I put my hand over the receiver and said to Esposito, "You never heard this conversation, you hear?"

Esposito said, "What conversation?"

"Tom, I think we got the guy, name's Ethan Dwyer. Can

you do something to pin his location to the crime scenes? I'm gonna need something to justify a search. Thanks, man. I owe you."

The rain beat on the windshield as Esposito drove. I asked him, "Where they got Dwyer?"

"Dwyer? It was some business guy named Delaney."

"Delaney?"

"I think so. You want me to check it?"

"No. You sure it isn't Dwyer?"

"It could be. I thought I heard Delaney."

"Where is he?"

"On ice downtown, holding him on evading arrest."

36

———

MY HEART WAS RACING AND MY NECK KILLING ME AS I talked with the sheriff. He said the suspect didn't have a record. When he started peppering me with questions I began playing it down a couple of octaves.

This guy, Delaney, was being held in a pen in the basement, and I told Chester I'd bring him up to speed after I interviewed him.

The elevator lurched down, and a flutter erupted in my belly. It had to be hunger—Luca didn't get nervous, did he? The doors parted, and I stepped onto a gray, concrete floor. I heard an officer say, "Save it for the judge. Now, move along."

An officer at a desk behind a gate said, "Hey Luca, heard what happened, man. You all right?"

"A little banged up, that's all. I guess I was pretty lucky."

"Thank god, I heard it was a pickup."

I nodded as I signed in, placing my gun on the counter.

"Shit, they're making these frigging pickups like tanks."

"Delaney out yet?"

"They just put him in interrogation room two."

"Thanks."

"Man, if I was you, I'd be taking a couple of weeks off."

I shrugged. "See you later, Tommy."

Looking through the small, wired glass window, I studied Thomas Delaney, and the flutter in my gut flared up. His jet-black hair was combed straight back, forming a widow's peak. The sleeves of his white shirt were rolled up and his hands were clasped. He looked like a Gordon Gekko Wall Streeter, not a serial killer.

Inhaling deeply, I opened the door. Delaney gave a weak smile as I limped to the seat opposite him.

"Detective Luca, the guy you almost killed."

"I—I didn't even know you got in an accident. I'm sorry, but I had no idea you were even trying to stop me."

Why did it always take several denials before the truth began to leak out?

"Where were you going, Mr. Delaney?"

"A friend's house."

"And from where?"

"Ah, work. I work at Wells Fargo, by Neapolitan."

"What do you do there?"

"I'm an analyst, you know, examine the financial statements of the companies we follow. See if any trends, positive or negative, can be identified."

"Sounds like a cure for insomnia."

"It can be mundane, but sometimes you find a nugget of information, and the pay is pretty good."

"You live in Pelican Bay?"

"Yes, I've got a coach home in Crestwood. Been there ten years."

They were nice units, just under two thousand square feet

and were going for six hundred and change. "You a religious man, Mr. Delaney?"

"Religious? I wouldn't call myself religious, but I believe there's a higher power, you know what I mean?"

"Nothing else makes sense to me. You go to church?"

He shook his head. "I used to, but now, only the holidays. I go to Saint Williams."

"You ever go to The Spirit of Fellowship Church up on Immokalee?"

"No, why?"

"Do you do any volunteer work?"

"I'm pretty busy, you know, but I care. I donate a fair sum each year to a bunch of places, St. Matthews, the Children's Fund, Habitat."

I held up a hand. "Okay."

Delaney leaned forward. "If I have to do some community service or something to make this go away, no problem. I'll do it."

"Help me to understand something here, Mr. Delaney. You're on your way to a friend's house, there's a torrential downpour, and your speeding through a yellow light. You seem pretty conservative, working as an analyst. Why were you in such a hurry?"

"I didn't know you were following me. Honestly, I didn't."

"Come on now, I don't like it when people lie to me. It's like they think I'm stupid."

"No, no, I don't think anything like that."

"Then why didn't you pull over?"

Delaney's shoulders sunk. "I don't want to lose my job. They'll fire me if they find out."

"As long as you didn't kill anyone, you've got nothing to worry about."

"Well, I've been dating this girl. We get along really well, and she, well, she likes to smoke marijuana. I don't smoke the stuff; I'm a bourbon guy. Anyway, she asked me to swing by a girlfriend of hers to pick up a small bag of the stuff."

"Is this stuff in the car?"

"No, I tossed it out the window."

The pain in my neck surged when I realized it was all because of a nickel bag of weed.

"Okay. I noticed the reverse lights on your Honda didn't seem to be working right."

"Yeah, there's some recall notice about it. I'm bringing it in next week."

Recall notice? Shit, I never thought to check into that.

"Would you voluntarily consent to a search of your car?"

"Absolutely, I have nothing to hide."

"Okay, I'll get the consent forms arranged, and if it's clean, we'll release you."

"It will be—I guarantee it."

"Okay, and do me a personal favor since I'm the one who got banged up. I'd appreciate if you'd consider donating to the Naples EMS."

"No problem. I'd be happy to do what I can. Really, no problem at all."

Before going to see Chester, I retreated to the bathroom. Trying to coax a urination out, I couldn't believe the position I was in. Not only was my damn neck and knee hurting, but I wrecked my car and reputation. How the hell was I gonna spin this? Thank God Haines had jumped the gun with Hannah, or Chester would have me working security at the courthouse.

Washing my hands, I realized there wasn't a viable excuse for my recklessness that made sense. Without a way to dress it up, I had no choice but to fess up to my mistake. I'm not sure where it came from, but it hit me that with Vargas in the hospital, and with the shine off the FBI, I was still Chester's best hope to solve this case.

37

———————

No one would describe me as cautious, but after being reminded by Chester that we had swung and missed twice, it was time to choke up on the bat. Tax records had a Robert DeBlasi as the owner of the Mangrove Bay home Ethan Dwyer had registered his Honda to. Either he was bunking with a friend, or it was a diversionary tactic.

Haines had pinged Dwyer's cell phone history, and it showed he was often around The Spirit of Fellowship Church. We had the Honda, a church connection, and his cell phone in the vicinity of three crime scenes the day before the bodies were discovered. Under normal circumstances, I'd have Dwyer sweating in an interrogation room, but I hesitated on pulling the trigger. It'd be nice to have Vargas around to run interference if I screwed up again. Three strikes you're out, but if no one was looking, you could get four.

Telling myself that going to see the owner of the house where Dwyer had his car registered wasn't violating every protocol, I headed to Mangrove Bay. Turning off Goodlette, I slowed down. My neck flared when I jammed the brake pedal. A thin man was getting into an Accord parked in the driveway. Considering whether to tail, I took my foot off the brake, pulled in back of him, and got out.

The Accord's driver door opened. Dwyer stuck his head out, threw his hands up, and got out. Grabbing his lower back, he arched back, lifting his chin toward a darkening sky. Scarecrow-like, Dwyer's green shirt looked like it was on a coat hanger, and his beige pants were bunched up at the waist. My suspect's brown hair was parted down the middle, like Johnny Depp, but not as long.

He was one of the guys who had been helping Minister Booth pack bags of food. "Mr. Dwyer?"

A gust of wind blew as he nodded. "Yes."

"Detective Luca, with the sheriff's office. You got a couple of minutes to talk?"

"Sure, what about?"

Pointing to a charcoal mass over the Gordon River, I said, "We might be better off inside."

"All right, come on in." As he reached in his car to hit the remote, I peered in the Honda's window: cloth seats and a wooden cross hanging from the rearview mirror.

The gray speckled floored two-car garage was completely empty, except two carpet runners with tire impressions and a stack of tile. Was Dwyer another neat freak?

The house had a fresh paint smell to it but no furniture other than two folding chairs and an aluminum folding table.

"You just move in?"

Holding the rear of the chair, he slowly lowered himself. "No, been here about ten months. It's not mine. It's my half-brother's home. About a month before they closed, his wife's appendix burst, and it's been one thing after another."

"Sorry to hear."

"She's doing better at the moment. We'll see how it goes. Anyway, he didn't want the house empty, and my lease was up, so I'm basically a house sitter. I inhabit the third bedroom."

Inhabit? "If you like the water, this is a great spot to be."

"I don't mind the beach, but you can keep the boating and fishing."

"You like to hunt?"

"A little, when I was up in Wisconsin."

Interesting. The state with the loosest gun laws in America. As far as I knew, you didn't need a permit for a rifle or a handgun.

"I love to hunt, got a bunch of rifles, 30.06, a Ruger 308, a Savage MK 11, and about five others."

I laughed.

"How about you? You own a couple?"

I gave him a blank look.

"What did you want to discuss?"

"I'll get right to it. You go to The Spirit of Fellowship Church, don't you?"

"I volunteer a couple of times a month. Minister Booth is genuine, if lax."

"What do you mean by that?"

"James 4:11 instructs us, 'Do not speak against a brother.'"

How the hell do they remember all these quotes? "Probably a good policy, but in my line of work, I depend on people talking." I laughed.

"Minister Booth is a good, God-loving man. He does a lot of good work. It's getting late, and I must get going."

"How do you like your Accord? I was thinking of getting one myself."

"It's good, I like it, but I don't care much about cars."

"I hear you. The only thing I care about is that it starts."

He smiled. "I feel the same."

"I was talking to a guy when I was getting gas, and he said there was a problem with the backup lights, something about a recall."

"Yeah, my reverse light is on most of the time. I have to make an appointment to get it rectified."

"It's funny. A car seen at a couple of the Aquatic Assassin crime scenes had the same issue."

"Is that why you're here? You think I'm the one who killed those . . . men?"

It was a curious pause. "We're just running down all the Accord owners in the county, and there's a helluva lot of them."

Narrowing his eyes, he asked, "Is this the point where you ask me where I was on the nights all the murders took place?"

"I don't like asking, but I gotta put something in the report to rule you out. I don't need much, say, one or two firm alibis would be enough to cross you off the list."

"I was probably working. I work most nights."

"Where are you working?"

"I drive for Uber mostly, but I do Lyft every now and then."

Shit. No wonder his cell phone records pinned him as being in the crime scene areas.

"Can you make any money doing that?"

"Depends. That's why I only drive late at night—less drivers on the road, so fares rise."

"Makes sense. Down here things start slowing down around eight."

"I never go out till nine, sometimes ten."

Before I could speak he followed up. "Not all the time; a lot of times I'm out by six, you know, take people to dinner. Some people use us to go home from work."

Which was it? Never before nine or by six?

"Sounds like a science. Just give me one day then so I can get out of here. How about the night of June twenty-fifth?"

"Let me think a moment. Oh yes, I was with my half-brother. He came down—there was an issue with the flooring. Some defect. They had to replace a lot of it, and he had to pick a replacement."

"Sounds like a nightmare. But with his wife sick, he came down? I know my girlfriend would've went nuts if I left her alone. Couldn't they just send him samples?"

"There was a lot of samples. They're in the garage, but yeah, I think he needed a break and wanted to come down. He has a lot of money tied up in this place."

"Thanks for clearing that up. Hey, you mind giving me a quick tour of this place? I don't know anybody with a house like this."

"Sure." He swung his legs to the side of the chair and grimaced.

"Back bothering you?"

"All the time."

"I got some exercises that help, you know, stretches. They really work."

He shook his head. "I have a steel rod in my back, fused vertebrae, smashed discs, you name it."

"Wow. What happened?"

"Hit by a damn drunk driver. Was in the hospital two months. Had to learn how to walk again and everything."

"Hope the bastard is behind bars."

"He had collected three DUIs before he struck my car, and all he received was a measly eighteen-month sentence. The judicial system failed miserably."

I was part of the system, and he was right. Sometimes there seemed to be a hand on the justice scale.

"This is the master suite. Wait till you see the bathroom—it's like a spa."

I liked the gray-and-white palette of the bathroom, but what really interested me was the bedroom area. There wasn't a piece of furniture in it.

38

―――――

"Is this Robert DeBlasi?"

"Yes, who's calling?"

"Detective Frank Luca, Collier County Sheriff's Office."

"Did something happen to my house?"

"No, I just have a couple of questions about your recent visit."

"I haven't been down in almost a year."

"Oh, maybe there's been some misunderstanding."

"What's this all about?"

"I understand your half-brother, Ethan Dwyer, is house-sitting for you."

"Yes, it's a long story, but my wife became ill, and we've had to postpone our move to Naples."

"You and Mr. Dwyer are half-brothers?"

"Not exactly, my parents took him in through the foster care program. He lost his mother at an early age. She was murdered, and he went through the system for about five years before he came to live with us."

"Nice of your parents. How did you get along with him?"

"Is Ethan all right? He didn't do something, did he?"

"Was he ever violent?"

"Violent? No. He was a bright kid, smarter than me, but he was guarded, kinda reserved. He never quite fit in. He started spending a lot of time at one of those evangelical churches. I thought the place was over the top, but Ethan said he liked the fire they had."

"Do you remember the name of the church or minister?"

"Geez, that was a long, long time ago. I can't remember that. Look, did he do anything that would get him in trouble?"

"It's a large investigation, and I'm looking at all kinds of possibilities. What else can you tell me?"

"Ethan had a very rough start but wasted his intelligence. He has a crazy high IQ, something over a hundred and thirty, but despite that, he bounced around from job to job. Never employed at anything meaningful. Ethan's a good guy, just lost, I guess you could say."

"Anything else?"

"Like I said, he was dealt a terrible hand as a kid, then he was hit by a drunk, and we almost lost him. He was really screwed up, needed a couple surgeries. It was a struggle for him to get back on his feet."

After finishing up with DeBlasi, I made another call.

"Tommy boy, it's Frank."

"Tommy boy?"

Caught red-handed trying to butter him up. "That's what I used to call a friend I grew up with, that's all."

"How'd you make out with the . . . information?"

"That's why I'm calling. It was helpful, but I could really use some help with something else."

"No problem. If I can help, I will."

"Can you get information from Uber and Lyft about a driver's activity? You know, where his rides originated and ended."

"These tech companies protect their data like crazy."

"Unless their selling it to an advertiser."

"No doubt. How many days of data you looking for?"

"I'm looking to see if a suspect was near the crime scenes, innocently driving someone, or not."

"If you don't need the passengers' names it will be easier."

"Not at all."

"Email the suspect's name and DMV records, and I'll see what I can do."

"Thanks, man. You're a lifesaver, bro."

39

MY GUILT WAS CROWDING OUT MY SYMPATHY. MARY ANN was rushed back into the hospital. I felt bad for her, I really did, but the timing couldn't be worse. I was going to meet Kayla for drinks at the Wine Loft in Mercato. It was selfish and childish, but I couldn't shake my self-centered desire to see her.

My watch read 5:50 when I pushed through the hospital's revolving door. I'd left work earlier than usual, scheming to stay with Mary Ann for an hour and a half, hoping I'd be able to scoot out and meet Kayla around seven thirty, as planned.

Mary Ann was eating when I walked in her room.

"You get a tray for me?"

"Hi, Frank. You're here early."

I pecked her cheek. "I was worried about you. You look good, and you're eating. You can't be feeling too bad."

"I don't have any pain. They gave me something as soon as I was admitted. They took some X-rays, and the doctor thinks it's a cyst on my right ovary."

"That's what they said last time, right?"

"Not the doctor, it was a nurse who said she had the same kind of pain."

"They should have checked it out then."

"I know, but anyway, tomorrow I'm getting an MRI, and if they confirm that's what's giving me trouble, I'll have a procedure the next day."

"You better eat good, then. I could grab a pie from Rosedale, because you're not going to be able to eat before the surgery."

The mush on her plate made me want to upchuck. I couldn't even look at it.

"You didn't eat, right?"

"No. But I'm okay."

"You want my applesauce?" She held up a hockey-puck-sized container.

"Nah. Maybe I'll see what they have in the cafeteria later."

"Give me an update on Dwyer."

By the time we finished talking about the case it was it six-thirty. We watched the news, and halfway through *Jeopardy* two of her girlfriends came in, laden with balloons and magazines. After a ten-minute greeting, I got two chairs for them and checked my phone.

"Frank, why don't you go?"

"No, it's okay." I said what I had to say instead of doing a fist pump.

"But you didn't eat yet, and it's almost seven thirty. Go get something to eat and go home. I'm fine."

"You sure? I don't want to leave you alone."

"We've got a lot of catching up to do."

"You're not going to be talking about me, are you?"

The girls giggled like cheerleaders.

Mary Ann said, "Go ahead. Get something to eat and go home. I'll see you tomorrow, okay?"

"You sure?"

"Bye, Frank."

I kissed all three on the cheek and resisted the temptation to skip out of the room. I hit the elevator button at 7:28. Perfect.

The elevator and my demeanor fell at the same time. A pianist was playing "The Girl Who Got Away" in the hospital's lobby. I pushed the guilt and the door out and headed to meet Kayla.

Driving toward 41, I cut into River Chase Plaza and jumped into a Publix supermarket. They always had flowers. I grabbed two bunches, checked out, and got back in the car.

The smell of lilies clogged up my nasals. Another oversight, Luca. Man, you're slipping. I debated what looked better, a bunch in each hand, or combining both. Opting for the visual of one large bouquet, I put a smile on and entered.

"Frank! I thought you went home."

"I couldn't leave you here with these two."

"He's a keeper, Mary Ann."

I said, "Let me get something from the nurse's station to put these in." I stepped outside and sent a text to Kayla that something had come up.

40

"WHAT DO YOU HAVE FOR ME, TOMMY?"

"Dwyer was driving for Uber each of the nights the victims were shot—"

"What?"

"Hold on, Frank. I'm getting to the interesting part. Uber has a couple of modes for drivers. One is the normal mode, where drivers are alerted about a person nearby looking for a ride. Dwyer was using that mode, which is the default option, when he started driving each of the days in question. Then he went dark, never accepted a ride for a while, then he went into what they call 'go home' mode. When a driver is at the end of his day and wants to head home he plugs in his destination, and the app looks for people who need a ride in that direction."

"Makes sense. I always wondered about how drivers work their way back home."

"Well, it seems Dwyer was masking his moves. Uber said they offered rides each of the nights in question that were heading in the direction Dwyer said he wanted to go, but Dwyer never accepted."

"Pretty cunning of him. What was the location Dwyer told Uber he wanted to go?"

"Downtown Fifth Avenue area."

"That's close to where he's staying. You have something hard we can bring to Sheriff Chester?"

"This was unofficial, Frank."

"I'm going to need something to get a warrant. We need to search his car and the Mangrove Bay house."

"Hm, that's going to be a problem. We go back to Uber, and they're gonna hide behind the privacy bullshit."

"Why don't you come down; tell the sheriff what Uber gave you?"

"You think that's going to make a difference?"

"We got nothing else to go with, besides, you have cred with him."

"Used to, Frank, used to. After the way I botched the Hannah thing—"

"Bullshit. You're with the Feds, the FBI. Chester will buy in."

"I don't share your optimism, but if you need me, I'll head down."

"Meet up in my office. I wanna unified front."

HAINES CAME into the office wearing blue slacks and a white short-sleeve shirt.

"Where's your jacket?"

"In the car. It's ninety out."

"Do me a favor. I know Chester; it'll play well with him. Go and get it."

Buttoning my top button, I pulled my tie tight, pinched the knot and put my jacket on. I didn't tell Chester that

Haines was coming with me. His eyes bounced between Tom and I before he smiled and got up.

We shook hands. "Good to see you, Tom, Frank. Sit. Take a seat. Frank didn't tell me you were coming."

I said, "Tom and I have been working closely. He's been very helpful."

Chester raised his eyebrows. "Good." Then he looked directly at me. "That's the way it's supposed to be. Any more mutual admiration we have to get through before you explain why you called this meeting?"

"We believe we have identified a suspect responsible for the serial killings." Chester leaned forward as I continued. "A thirty-nine-year-old male Caucasian named Ethan Dwyer, a volunteer at The Spirit of Fellowship Church."

Chester shook his head. "What do you have on him?"

"Cell phone records that place Dwyer at each of the crime scenes on the nights in question."

"Calls?"

"No, cell tower pings. They're not exact, but you can't argue with five out of five."

"It's not my job to argue, Luca. I leave that for the defense attorneys, and they'd poke more than enough holes in it. I'm hoping that's not all you have."

Haines said, "I'm not disputing the range involved with towers, but we've been able to establish some triangulation involving two of the crime scenes that are going to be difficult to explain away. I'm not an attorney, but this level of location data is fairly precise. It's worked in more than a few cases we've handled on the federal level."

"Okay, that's a little stronger." Chester beckoned with his hand. "Give me more."

"In an informal interview with Dwyer, I asked about his whereabouts on the night of the Chapman murder. He gave me a story he was with his brother, really a half-brother, that turned out to be bull."

"I don't have to tell you, people lie all the time to cover things they don't want to surface."

Rather than ask Chester if he thought I got to be his lead homicide detective by being a moron, I took a breath and continued.

"Upon presenting Mr. Dwyer with the cell phone location information, we, actually Tom and the FBI had developed, Dwyer said he was an Uber driver and driving every night. In trying to verify his whereabouts, I reached out to Agent Haines. Tom, would you take it from here?"

Haines crossed his legs. "Detective Luca was rightly concerned about how to defend against a claim that the suspect was driving around for work. We discussed it, and I have some unofficial contacts that definitely dispute any claim he was providing transportation for Uber clients."

"Unofficial?"

"The bureau has a lot of interaction with Uber and other technology firms. Publicly, these firms have policies that require going through a protracted court battle before they eventually capitulate. In cases like this, where time is of the essence and lives are at stake, the bureau has developed an unofficial back channel to obtain the information needed."

"Dwyer was lying again. He wasn't working at the time of the killings."

"We'll need to prove this. Are you going to be able to get Uber to back this up, officially?"

Haines said, "I'm afraid not quickly. It will take several weeks, if not months."

"Sir, if I may. We may not need to. What we'd like is your help in securing a warrant. With a search of Dwyer's car and home we hope to discover hard, incriminating evidence."

Chester put up a palm. "This comes down to Dwyer lying about an alibi, and you think a judge will sign off on a warrant?"

Haines said, "It goes a bit deeper than simply lying about an alibi. This involves him being at each of the crime scenes on the nights in question."

"At or near?"

"Near several, and about as close to *at* as you could be on both the Cornwall and Parker scenes."

"I don't think we have enough."

Haines said, "I understand, and I'm not disputing the right to operate on different standards, but as far as the bureau goes, we'd have enough."

"Sir, if I may, I'd like to add to what Agent Haines said. This case is the most notorious case we've ever experienced in Southwest Florida. I can't imagine a judge turning down our request for a search."

Chester said, "Did you forget about Levin? That old goat hinders my department at every turn."

"We can bring it to Crown or Carr. Either of them will sign it."

Haines said, "If there is a judge who would be open to, uh, an informal recommendation from the bureau, it could be a deciding factor."

"You know how judges feel about interference. It could taint our effort. I'll leave it to the DA to draft his request."

"Sir, we've got to do this now. We believe the shooter fired from inside his car. The presence of any gunshot residue in the car is degrading as we speak."

41

Usually I love smacking a warrant on a suspect's chest, but though I believed Dwyer could be the killer, I hadn't developed a hatred of him. All he was at this point was a damn liar. It'd be interesting to see his reaction.

Two officers scurried to cover the rear doors as a light in the house next door came on.

As a line of light cracked across the horizon, I knocked on the door and turned around.

"Collins! Hook the Honda up and tow it downtown. Mulroney's waiting for it."

I felt the door swinging toward me and thrust the warrant at a bare-chested Dwyer, who shook his head in disbelief.

"What are you doing with my car?"

Staring at a large scar that swung toward his back, I said, "We have a warrant to search the premises and impound your vehicle."

Dwyer stepped out of the house, pulling a ratty pair of gym shorts up to a nonexistent hip. "What the heck are you looking for?"

Heck? When we storm your house at six a.m.? "Step aside, Mr. Dwyer."

With a concave chest and bony knees, he looked like some of the people in my oncologist's waiting room.

"You expect me to stand out here with no shirt or shoes? What is this, Russia?"

"Show me to your bedroom. You can get dressed, and then you'll stay outside with Officer Brown."

"This is bullshit. You're wasting your time."

His tone was all wrong. It was forced. Dwyer was hiding something, but what? As far as I knew, there wasn't a stereotype look for serial killers, but he looked as far from one as you could get. Was he dealing drugs? Hiding a theft of some kind?

Dwyer's bedroom was puzzling. Along one wall, there were evenly spaced shoes lined up terminating at a knee-high pile of flip-flops and sneakers. Dwyer swung a pair of bifold doors open, revealing a wardrobe that was organized by the color and height of the garments hanging in it.

Dwyer grabbed a pair of jeans and grunted as he sorted through a pile of tee shirts in a plastic bin, pulling one with a saxophone pictured on it. He went to retrieve his phone and wallet from the top of a whitewashed dresser that had stacks of coins in equal height.

Pulling on a glove, I said, "You'll have to leave those behind. Hand me those clothes."

"But you said I can get dressed."

"You can, but I need to go through them first."

I patted down the clothes and watched him get dressed before handing him off to Officer Brown.

A pile of dirty clothing, piled in the corner, revealed nothing but left me wondering if there was a functioning laundry room in the house. I thumbed through his wallet. A

Visa card, driver's license, library card, and three old pictures of a woman I assumed was his mother. I put it back down and bagged the phone, which had a cracked screen.

A drawer-by-drawer search yielded nothing but a dozen bottles, most of them empty, of Tylenol PM and clothing. There had to be a place Dwyer kept his paperwork, like his birth certificate, diplomas, passport.

The top of a nightstand that screamed IKEA had a King James Bible, an *Understanding the Bible's True Meaning*, a three-inch book tagged with scores of sticky notes, three differently colored highlighters, and matching pads of Post-its. I opened the Bible's companion to a pink sticky about halfway down.

Highlighted in pink were two passages:

Isaiah 43:10, 11: You are my witnesses, declares the Lord, and my servant whom I have chosen, that you may know and believe me and understand that I am he.

And,

Psalms 143:10: Teach me to do your will, for you are my God!

I reread the passages, thumbed through the rest of the book, and put it down gently. As soon as I slid the night-stand's drawer open I saw a dull brass key that screamed safety deposit box. I shot a photo of it and bagged the key.

Even though the house was empty, it still took us time to check for hiding spots. It was early, but there was no way I was going up in the attic. That was a job for one of the younger cops, like Soto. It was our last chance to find something concrete, otherwise my hopes were resting on the car and phone we seized.

Soto pulled down the garage's attic stairs and disappeared into the darkness armed with a neon flashlight.

His footsteps grew fainter as he searched the far corners

of the attic. I wanted to radio him to see what was going on. We needed the gun.

Finally, a leg appeared looking for a step, and a sweat-darkened Soto made his way down.

"Nothing but a dead palm rat up there. All foam insulation, but nothing, even under the AC unit."

"Okay, thanks. A little hot up there, huh?"

"Like an oven, man."

"All right, let's rap this up. Boaz, give a receipt to Dwyer and tell Brown we're through here."

***

VARGAS WAS MOVING GINGERLY when she came in around ten. Her pants were loose, and I wondered if she'd lost a bra size as well.

"About time you showed up, Vargas. Just like you to use a little surgery as an excuse to take three days off."

"I was going to say it's good to be back, but I'm reconsidering."

"How you feeling?"

"Okay. Got some pinching going on over here." She pointed to her lower abdomen.

"That's where the ovary is, right?"

"Yep, they said to expect it, but that doesn't make it any more comfortable. I couldn't sit around. I need something to distract me."

"Well, you've come to the right place. I'm really glad you're back." I pulled her chair back. "I could use the help talking this Dwyer guy over—"

Vargas shuffled over. "Let's get to it, then."

As she lowered herself into the chair, I said, "They were

able to detect trace elements of gunshot residue from the passenger door."

"So, he shot out the passenger window."

"Let's see him explain that away. And Dwyer's phone was used to call three of the five victims. Two of them several times."

"I don't know. That sounds weak. No texts?"

"Nada. This guy is smart. Why would he use his phone to make contact with them?"

"Maybe they were related to his volunteering at the church. It'd be better if there were all five on it, but I don't think it means anything much, Frank."

"But two calls were made just hours before Chapman and Cornwall ended up dead. He was probably calling them to set a meet-up."

"Last night you mentioned a key that looked like it was to a safety deposit box."

"I got FCU checking to see if they can identify the bank. I'm hoping that's where we find the gun."

"If the banks knew how many guns were hidden in their boxes, they'd think twice about it."

"Who you kidding? You think they don't know?"

Vargas shrugged. "We'll need a warrant for the box if that's what the key is to. You said there was no paperwork at all in the house. That's real odd."

"I know, but this Dwyer is an oddball to begin with. I'm hoping it's not just filled with paperwork."

"You think we should bring Dwyer in, or wait to see what's what with the lockbox?"

"I'd like to wait a day, make him feel comfortable; see if we can find the bank box."

My email box pinged. I said, "The forensics report is in. I'll forward it to you."

"Good."

"Holy shit! The glasses!"

"What's going on?"

"A pair of glasses were found under the passenger seat."

"Yeah?"

I picked up the phone. "They could be Bobby Hagan's. He couldn't see shit without glasses, had some condition uval or whatever. Get out the Hagan file."

"But he was found floating in the Gulf. Kinda tough to keep your glasses on."

"This is Detective Luca—the Dwyer case. A pair of glasses were found in the subject's car. I need a reading on the prescription in the lenses. And I need it now. Can you do that? If not, I'll be down to pick up the evidence and run it over to Lenscrafters."

42

Dwyer had a smirk on his face when we walked into the room. Trailing Vargas as she carefully made her way to the table, my father's voice flooded my head: *I'm going to knock that smirk off your face, Frankie.* Dad could be tough, but it'd only last an hour, max. I didn't realize it then, but I learned a ton about life from him. I felt cheated; he had a heart attack at forty-eight and was gone.

I scraped my plastic chair forward as Vargas recited the formalities for the record. She said, "Mr. Dwyer, you are aware that you're entitled to be represented at this interview by an attorney?"

"Yes, I'm aware."

"And you are declining to exercise that right?"

"Yes."

"You're aware that should you be unable to afford an attorney, the public defender's office will provide representation to protect your interests?"

"I don't need one. Besides, having counsel would make me appear guilty."

I said, "Mr. Dwyer, you're the owner of a brown, 2015

Honda Accord, registered under Florida plate number XLR309?"

He raised a bony finger. "Yes, but you got the plate number wrong. It's XRL, not XLR."

I checked my notes. "Yes, that's correct, I inverted the letters. Your car, the Accord, was impounded and searched. I'd like to ask you about what we found."

"Be my guest."

"The passenger door, sill, and armrest had trace elements of gunshot residue."

Dwyer leaned to the right. "Gunshot residue? How did that get there?"

"That's our question. Just how did it get there? Did you fire a gun from inside the car?"

"No."

"Did someone else fire a gun from inside the vehicle?"

"Not that I'm aware of."

"How do you explain it, then?"

Dwyer changed his lean to the left. "Perhaps your forensics people were mistaken, confusing whatever substance they found with gunshot residue."

Sliding a piece of paper across the table, I said, "This is the report from an electron microscope. As detailed, the X-ray spectrometry evidences the presence of lead, antimony, and barium in proportions consistent with the characteristics of gunshot residue."

Dwyer studied the report. There was no way he could read the report. He was buying time.

"The barium and antimony particle counts are barely in the acceptable range. It's a questionable report." He flicked the document back to me.

"Barely or not, it's in the range. The residue originated from a firearm."

"Again, questionable. It could simply be from my car's brake linings. That is a more logical conclusion to make, in my opinion."

What the fuck? Brake linings did have similar profiles, but that proved nothing. "I'm not here to debate the findings."

"I believe it was you who brought up the report."

Vargas said, "Your phone, which was seized during the search, logged calls between you and several of the victims."

"Define several, please."

Vargas cleared her throat. "Chapman and Cornwall."

"Several is the wrong determiner. Several is used only when there are more than two."

"Thanks for the English lesson, my friend. Answer the lady's question."

"I'm sorry, Detective, but it wasn't a question, just a statement."

Dwyer was a wiseass but polite about it. "Let me rephrase. You had several calls with two of the victims. What was the nature of those conversations?"

"I don't recall precisely, but I'm an active volunteer at The Spirit of Fellowship Church and met both men there. I'm certain the calls were related to the ministries I'm involved in."

"Did those ministries also put you in contact with Shaun Parker, Brett Tinder, and Bobby Hagan?"

Dwyer stroked a chin that was sharp enough to cut his fingers. "I believe they work at the church. I'm just a volunteer. I see them around the church, and at times we work together."

"I'll take that as a yes. You knew all five men?"

"To varying degrees."

"You knew Chapman and Cornwall good enough to talk

over the phone. How well did you know the others, for example, Bobby Hagan?"

Dwyer scrunched his face up and arched his shoulders. "Not well. We hardly knew each other."

"Hm. That's interesting. You hardly knew Bobby Hagan."

"That's correct."

"How do you explain that we found his glasses in your car?"

Dwyer grimaced, put his hands on the edge of the chair, and shifted. "My back stiffens when I sit in one position too long."

Vargas said, "Would you like to take a break and stretch?"

"That would be wonderful."

Dwyer stood, put his hands on the table and arched his back as Vargas spoke into the mic, "The interview of Ethan Dwyer is being paused."

Vargas clicked off the recording device, and I followed her out the room.

"This prick thinks he's smarter than us."

"What was that with the GSR report? Did he work as a scientist or something?"

"No, but his brother said he had a high IQ, over one thirty."

"And he's driving for Uber?"

"You know what I say, 'Genius and madness are a hair away from each other.'"

"Dwyer is hardly mad, Frank. In fact, he's not only under control but seems confident."

"We go back in and go hard at him. Knock him off his game."

Vargas nodded. "You want a coffee?"

"Yeah. Hey, how's your tummy?"

"I don't know if it's the distraction, but it actually feels better."

"Super. You wanna ask Mr. Ivy League if he wants something? He'll probably ask for a damn Perrier."

Vargas flicked a switch and said, "Resuming the interview of Ethan Dwyer by Detectives Vargas and Luca." Turning to Dwyer, she said, "Feeling better now?"

"Yes, I appreciate the opportunity to stretch."

I said, "Back to the glasses. How did Bobby Hagan's glasses end up under the passenger seat of your car?"

A vein near Dwyer's temple pulsed. "I don't know. I could speculate that he probably dropped them."

"Bobby Hagan was a passenger in your 2015 Honda Accord?"

"I provided him with a lift or two."

Vargas said, "Where did you take Mr. Hagan?"

"I don't remember specifically, but it had to do with church business."

I said, "Hagan dropped them while in your car. Is that right?"

"It's the likely scenario."

"And when you drove him to wherever you were going, he got out and left his glasses behind?"

"It's a reasonable explanation."

"Bobby Hagan had a vision disorder known as uveal coloboma. Without his glasses he was almost blind. There's no way Hagan leaves his glasses behind. Oh, there is one way, if he was forced, say with a gun to his head, I suppose he'd leave everything behind."

"I can't answer for the actions of anyone but myself."

"Did you see Bobby Hagan drop or take his glasses off?"

"He was constantly taking them off, cleaning them with a microfiber cloth."

"Would you agree that it is unusual for someone who is virtually blind without glasses to leave them behind?"

"People do all types of unusual things. Perhaps he had a second pair with him."

I'm a homicide detective. I hardly need the reminder. We played verbal ping-pong for another half hour but got nowhere. We had the gunshot residue, a couple of calls, and Hagan's glasses. We needed more. When I told him we were done for the day, Dwyer's smirk morphed into a smile.

We escorted Dwyer out of the building, watching the stick figure get into an Uber before I said, "We find that safety deposit box, and that smile is gonna vanish."

43

———————

I FELT LIKE WE'D FINALLY CAUGHT A BREAK; THE GUYS IN THE Financial Crimes Unit had identified the key as the type used by First Integrity Bank. They had only four branches in Naples. After eliminating a branch on Pine Ridge, we arrived at their Anchor Rode Drive branch in Park Shore. Heads turned and a buzz of whispers circled as Vargas, I, and a uniformed officer walked past the tellers to the administrative section.

The branch manager's eyes darted across the bank's main floor when he was shown the warrant. He quickly escorted us to a small waiting area out of view of his clients. The manager tapped onto a terminal. "Ethan Dwyer, box 9012. Right this way."

He punched a keypad, unlocking a door that led to a room whose three sides were lined with steel boxes. Dwyer's was to the left side of the rear wall, six from the floor. Digging in his pocket, the manager produced a shiny key that he inserted and turned. The box's small door swung open, and he slid out a ten-inch square box that had its own lock, placing it on the room's narrow table.

"Shall I wait outside?"

Vargas said, "No, please observe."

The officer pulled a hand drill out of his bag, checked the lock, and fitted an appropriate bit. It took less than thirty seconds to pop the lock out. The officer stepped aside.

Vargas and I exchanged glances before I slowly lifted the top off. A passport in a baggie topped a wad of documents. There didn't seem to be a gun or weapon of any kind. Scooping up the contents, I spread them on the table, whispering, "No damn gun."

Dwyer's car loan and title documents were in a plastic sleeve. Handing them to Vargas, I pawed through Dwyer's college and high school diplomas before uncovering a thick blue envelope in a Ziploc bag. Several bundles that appeared to be memorabilia were inside the envelope. A clip held twenty or so photos of Dwyer as a baby and young child. In each shot he was with his mother. The next bundle contained newspaper clippings. I opened them.

A picture of a woman, who had to be Dwyer's mother, stared at me under a headline that read, "Green Bay Woman Raped, Tortured, and Murdered." Scanning the article, there it was—Darlene Dwyer. The thirty-four-year-old was Dwyer's mom.

Two other articles in the bunch told the story of the search for Darlene Dwyer's killer. A lump surfaced in my throat when I read another headline: "Tortured Woman's Son Now Ward of State."

A clipping, folded like a napkin, opened into the front page of the *Green Bay Press*. The headline read, "Killer Caught in Madison." I swept my eyes over the page, pointed to the article and said, "Vargas, check this out."

"What about it?"

"Hagan. I'll bet this is Bobby Hagan's father. This could be some type of revenge killing."

"But there are four other corpses."

"There's got to be a connection."

There was one other article, and it covered a car wreck. There was a tiny picture of a helicopter on the interstate. Though it didn't mention any names, it had to be the one involving a drunk driver and Dwyer.

"This Dwyer likes collecting bad news. I don't know about you, Vargas, but I'd never hold on to this stuff."

"He's had some tough luck."

"And so have we. I really thought we were gonna find the murder weapon."

"Me too. Since the warrant was limited to the gun, let's grab some pictures of these."

***

VARGAS WASN'T CONVINCED of the connection to Hagan, believing it was purely coincidental. Her strongest arguments had to do with the length of time that had elapsed and that Hagan was victim number five. If he was a target, why not kill him first? They were excellent questions, but I had nothing else.

Afraid Vargas's devil advocacy would sway Chester, I told her to rest and climbed the stairs to see the sheriff. With each step, my doubts grew. It was beginning to feel like I was chasing a ghost, not a killer.

Chester put down a document and rose, offering a smile and a hand.

"Good to see you, Detective."

"Same here, sir."

"What do you have?"

I didn't want to ruin the mood he was in. "There's got to be a connection with Hagan's father killing Dwyer's mother. I want to bring Dwyer back in, explore that line."

"I tend to agree with you, but that was thirty years ago."

"He was a kid when it happened, fifteen to twenty years before he could do anything. Agent Haines said it wasn't unusual to wait a long time in a revenge case."

"He did?"

No, he didn't. "Yeah, something like, there's two types of revenge killings—those who go right at it, and those that plan, festering as they do."

"The only good revenge is one that's gone too far."

What? Was Chester stealing my quotes? "I like that, sir."

"And why would Dwyer kill the others? And not Hagan first?"

"We're looking into the victims' backgrounds and any cross sections with Dwyer."

"Didn't you already explore those possibilities?"

"Yes. But we're taking a closer look. See if any connections weren't obvious. I'm hoping another interview with Dwyer will help."

"Things have been quiet since the Hagan murder. Maybe Dwyer's gone cold because you're looking at him or he's done. Either way, I could get used to life as it was before this all started."

"Me too."

"Bring him in, and see what you get. We've got nothing to lose."

I rose. "Thank you, sir."

"How's Detective Vargas feeling?"

"She's doing well, sir. It's good to have her back."

"Good. You know, you two make a good couple."

What? "Uh, couple?"

Chester smiled. "Guess I meant partners."

What did Chester mean by that? Did he find out about Mary Ann and me? I didn't need anything else to think about. Damn, if they knew, we'd be forced to work different shifts. Then who'd help me with this case?

———

WE OBSERVED Ethan Dwyer through the window on the interrogation room's door. Vargas said, "This guy has been through a lot in his life. If he did it, he's got a lot of reasons for going off the rails."

"There's no reason to kill someone. I don't care what you've been through."

Dwyer unbuttoned a shirt button and Vargas said, "I thought you said you didn't raise the air-conditioning."

"I—I didn't."

Vargas shook her head. "It's been twenty minutes. You want to start now?"

"Give it another ten. I'm going to take a pee."

"That means twenty. Go ahead, I'll grab a coffee."

When we swung open the door, Vargas wagged her head. It was a good ten degrees warmer in the room.

"Uh, let me turn down the air. Sorry about that, Mr. Dwyer."

Call me crazy, but I enjoyed making suspects uncomfortable. It tilted the atmosphere in my favor.

Vargas and Dwyer were laughing when I came back in. "You want to let me in on the joke?"

Vargas said, "It's nothing, Frank, uh, Detective Luca."

"She asked me if I wanted a drink. It reminded me about how I used to make sure I had a sufficient amount of chocolate syrup for my milk while in foster care."

Pulling out a chair, I mumbled, "Sounds fascinating." Vargas shot me a dirty, make that a filthy look, and recited the formalities into the mic.

Dwyer had a blue shirt on with a tiny stain in the belly button area. I said, "We wanted to ask you some questions concerning what we found in the safety deposit box you keep at First Integrity on Anchor Rode."

"If you would have had the decency to ask, I would have granted you access to my safety deposit box."

"That's not the way it works with a warrant, Mr. Dwyer."

"I have nothing to hide, Detective. I'm afraid you're wasting your time on me."

"Thanks for your concern. Now, as you know, there were several newspaper articles relating to the murder of your mother."

Dwyer blinked at the word mother but volunteered nothing.

Vargas said, "It must have been traumatic, losing your mother at such a young age."

Dwyer nodded, pulling his lips in. "Unimaginable, an absolute nightmare. I was only eight. My mother was everything. My entire world—gone." He snapped his fingers. "just like that."

"I'm sure it was difficult."

"Difficult? Do you know what it's like to go from a loving, secure home into a seedy barrack where you must fend for yourself, or you'd be eating scraps in your damn underwear?"

"I wasn't trying to make light of the situation you were in,

Mr. Dwyer. I'm certain it was indescribable to anyone who wasn't there."

Dwyer scowled and picked at a fingernail.

"If we could concentrate on your mother's killer, Paul Hagan. His son, Bobby, was found floating in the Gulf of Mexico."

"I heard."

"That's quite a coincidence, isn't it?"

"What?"

"That the son of the man who murdered your mother is someone you knew and is now dead."

"Are you inferring that I'm a vigilante?"

"Vigilante. That's a good way to put it."

Dwyer exhaled. "Look, my mother died a long time ago. The man who tortured and killed her was arrested and incarcerated. I couldn't do anything about it."

"You were only eight at the time."

"Oh, so you believe I've been harboring this desire to atone for my mother's murder for thirty years and finally acted upon it?"

"Certainly would explain a lot of things, wouldn't it, Detective Vargas?"

Vargas said, "You moved down here fifteen or so years ago?"

"Yes, that's close enough."

She said, "Was that to follow Paul Hagan?"

"No, of course not."

Vargas followed with, "Just another coincidence then that Bobby Hagan moved to Florida only a year before you did?"

"Look, I moved after recovering from my accident." Dwyer leaned forward. "Do you know what I went through? Do you? Hospitalized for six months, couldn't walk. I was a damn mess, my back aching constantly. I needed a warm climate." He settled back. "My doctor said it would help with joint pain."

Vargas said, "I understand; it makes sense. But how did you come to meet Bobby Hagan?"

"He worked at the church. That's where I met him."

"How did you settle on The Spirit of Fellowship Church? It's not exactly around the corner."

He laughed. "It's a bit out of the way, but a small price to pay for God."

I said, "You want to tell us how you found the church?"

"It was recommended to me by a friend who said Minister Booth gave good sermons and was an inspiring man."

I said, "That's another heck of a coincidence."

"That's the difference between us believers. Nonbelievers like to classify things as coincidental, but I believe it is the hands of God. He put me there to be inspired by Minister Booth."

"He's quite an impressive figure, isn't he?"

"Minister Booth is what I call an awakener. He stirs you up, gets to the root of what God wants us to do. I just wish he was more proactive."

"How so?"

"Let's just say he talks a better game than he plays."

"I don't understand."

"God tells us not to speak evil of our brothers. Timothy 5:19, 'Do not admit a charge against an elder.'"

What is it, Dwyer? You like the minister or not? I said, "How soon after moving down here did you join The Spirit of Fellowship Church?"

"I don't know, a couple of months or so."

"How well did you know Chapman, Tinder, Cornwall, Parker, and Hagan?"

"I told you the last time you asked."

"Tell us again."

"I'm trying to cooperate, really I am, but this is bordering on being ridiculous." Dwyer carefully rose.

"Where you going?"

"My back is acting up, and I'm done with this. If you choose to continue this harassment, I'll retain counsel."

44

—————

"THIS GUY'S GOT BALLS. WALKING OUT OF AN INTERVIEW."

"He has a legal right to be represented. Frankly, I'm surprised with all the attention we've been giving him that he never got a mouthpiece."

"This guy's an enigma. I know you feel bad for the way his life turned out, but that's no excuse. There's something going on with him."

"Don't take this the wrong way, but do you think it's him because we have no one else?"

"No. Of course not, besides, we never cleared Hannah Booth."

Vargas said, "Let's chart this out." She got out of her chair and grabbed her side.

"You all right?"

"Yeah, just got up too quickly."

"You sure?"

"Yeah, it's been feeling good."

Grabbing a marker, Vargas wrote Dwyer in capital letters. She said, "What do we have that's hard evidence? Gunshot residue inside his car." She wrote *GSR* under Dwyer.

"And his car type was seen by two witnesses."

"That's not hard, Frank. There are thousands of Accords in the county."

Vargas drew a vertical line next to *GSR* and put *Accord* on the right side of the line.

"Hagan's glasses found in Dwyer's car is as hard as it gets."

"No doubt, unless we discover he carried a spare pair around with him."

"Why would he leave a pair behind? Dwyer probably put a gun to his head and Hagan panicked. Rushing out of the car, they fell off his face."

"It's possible. We've got to find out who his eye doctor was, and if and when he got new glasses."

"His condition—I wonder if it gets worse over time. If so, an old pair of glasses wouldn't be good anymore."

"Good point. We need to check into it." Vargas wrote *victim's glasses* under *GSR*. Now, we've got a couple of calls and contact with the victims through the church." She wrote *knew all victims* on the left, beneath *victim's glasses*.

My stomach growled. "Hagan's father killed his mother. Can't get harder than that."

"It's a connection that's difficult to explain, but we need something to prove it was revenge, and then we'd have to discover the motivations for the other killings."

"Maybe he was providing cover."

"Kill four others for cover?"

I knew it was ridiculous, but the facts were showing we had nothing concrete on Dwyer.

"He moved down here within months of Hagan moving."

"Hagan was in Wisconsin before that?"

"Yeah, just like Dwyer."

"Why would he wait until Hagan moved to kill him?"

"Man, I wish I knew. He could've tried, you never know."

"You think we should take another look at Hannah Booth?"

I shrugged.

"We've got her hair on a vic, and the gun used in two killings was found in her office. That's miles more than we have on Dwyer."

"But when the last killing happened she was sitting in a Lee County cell."

"A, with the time of death, muddled by Hagan floating in the Gulf, she could've killed him and then got herself drunk. Drown out what she just did. And B, maybe we have two killers. Hannah Booth killed the first four and Dwyer the fifth."

I'd never considered that. Vargas one-upped me again. "Maybe Dwyer saw the heat on Hannah and used that to even the score with Hagan. It's worth exploring, but don't forget the second gun was used to kill Parker too."

"I forgot about that."

Score one for Luca. "Maybe Hannah used two guns. Dwyer was around the church a lot and had access to Hannah's office." It was a stupid thought. "Why don't we look at any connections he might have had with Parker. Maybe it was Hannah for three and Dwyer for two."

"That would be crazy, Frank."

"Crazy is the business we're in, sunshine."

Vargas's face lit up with a smile that'd been missing since she'd been sick.

"Let's grab something to eat. I'm starving. What do you say we pick up sandwiches from Dolce & Salato and sit on a bench by the beach?"

AFTER LUNCH, Vargas headed to the coroner to discuss the time of death, and I worked the phone.

"Mrs. Hagan? It's Detective Luca, remember me?"

I was hoping she'd say something like, 'Sure, you're the one who looks like George Clooney,' but she said, "Hi there. I'm guessing this is about Bobby?"

"Yeah, I'd like to ask you a couple of questions."

"Listen, sweetie, I told you when you were here I didn't have much contact with him."

"I know, but it's concerning his eyesight. As his mother you'd know the most about it."

"His eyesight? The uveal coloboma condition?"

"Yes. Did he have to see an eye doctor regularly?"

"He should have been going at least once a year. I used to be on his back about it."

"Did his prescription change? Did he get new glasses a lot?"

"Sometimes he needed new glasses, but not all the time."

"Do you know which eye doctor he used?"

"You don't seem to understand, honey, I don't much see Bobby anymore."

"I understand. Last question. I promise. Who was the eye doctor you used to take him to?"

"Dr. Brower, over at the Coastland Mall. He'd be over seventy, if he's still around."

It was a long shot, but even if Hagan changed doctors they may have a record of who they transferred records to. Instead of calling, I hopped into the car, hoping to avoid having an eighteen-year-old receptionist try to blow me off.

45

———

Walking through Macy's to get to my car, I rolled around what Hagan's ophthalmologist said when Vargas called. I quickened my pace as she spoke, "Frank, Hagan's time of death isn't firm."

"What changed?"

"Coroner missed the fact that Hagan was taking blood pressure medicine."

"What does that have to do with it?"

"He was taking a beta blocker, and they slow down digestion."

Stepping into the sunshine, I said, "I didn't know that. What's the bottom line then?"

"Because Hagan was in the water, he based the TOD on the state of digestion from Hagan's last meal, a Whopper from Burger King. But now he's moved the TOD back two to three hours. Hannah Booth had more than enough time to kill Hagan, get smashed, and arrested for DUI."

"We're gonna need to replot the time line, make sure what we have here. You headed back?"

"No, I'm due in court in an hour."

"I'll see you later, then."

"Okay. You get anything from the eye doctor?"

"Yeah. Hagan was in a month ago, got new glasses. They were doing a buy one, get one free thing to compete with Vision Works, and Hagan got two pairs."

"He could've just dropped them in Dwyer's car, then."

"Yep."

TOSSING MY JACKET ON A CHAIR, I ripped off my tie and studied the board. I took the pin out of the picture of Hannah Booth and stared at it. Was I wrong about her? Was she really someone who could plan five murders without leaving much evidence? I pinned her photo next to Dwyer's and sat.

What about her son? Did he really die of an overdose, or was it suffocation? It might be easier to clarify her status by getting to the bottom of that death. If we exhumed the body, pinning a murder on Hannah, the other cases could come together.

Serial killers were overwhelmingly thirty-to-forty-year-old males. Who was the last female serial killer? I remembered that Wuornos lady, a Florida hooker who ended up killing seven of her johns in the eighties. Tapping at my keyboard, a list of females who'd committed multiple murders came up. Scrolling down, I was surprised at the number of them, but most of these killers committed their crimes in the twentieth century.

Closing the browser, I swiveled back to the board. Hannah was not only in the suspect pool but was in the deep end with Dwyer. Was it either one of them, or both? I remember laughing at Haines when he said the killer was intelligent. These two were frigging Einsteins at this point, and I had to find a way to give them a failing grade. Grabbing the phone, I put on my cheeriest voice,

"Minister Booth, it's Det . . . uh, Frank Luca."

"Hello Frank. How are you?"

"Doing well. Do you have a couple of minutes?"

"Well, I'm kind of busy."

"It's not about Hannah, but Ethan Dwyer."

"Oh, sure."

"When we spoke the last time, I don't think I asked about his relationship with Shaun Parker."

"I don't believe you did. What would you like to know?"

"Did they get along?"

"Yes, I believe so. Why do you ask?"

"I'm unable to discuss an active case, but I trust you enough to say there is strong evidence one of the victims was killed for revenge."

"Oh my God, that's terrible, holding such anger against another individual."

"Are you sure they got along?"

"Yes. We're blessed with a close-knit group of people here."

He must have forgotten about his wife's book throwing. "It seems that way, and you're to be commended, Minister, but we humans are built in such a way that we can't agree on everything. Why don't you give this a little more thought, see if you can recall anything between them?"

"Differences of opinion happen, but the key is to respectfully disagree. There's absolutely no reason to be nasty about it."

"I'm afraid we're losing that ability."

"With God's help, we'll reverse the tide."

I heard myself say, "Amen."

"I'm sorry, Detective, but I have to get going."

"Thank you for your time."

Playing over our conversation, I wondered if he was hiding anything. If he was covering anything, it wouldn't help his wife. Maybe he was concerned about how it would reflect on his church. A large part of his mission was directed toward giving people second and third chances. The publicity from a murderer in the midst of the church's activities would dry up his funding. Then, how would they pay off the money they borrowed? He had a million-dollar reason to keep quiet, but was that what was going on?

I GRABBED a cup of java and made my next call.

"Robert DeBlasi? This is Detective Luca. We spoke about your brother Ethan."

"Hi, by the way, Detective, Ethan is technically my foster brother. I think I told you my parents took him out of foster care."

"Yes, I remember. I've got a question or two for you."

"Go ahead."

"Does the name Shaun Parker mean anything to you?"

"Vaguely rings a bell. I think there was a family who used to live a couple of blocks away named Parker when we were growing up."

"Did they have any boys?"

"I think so, if my memory serves me."

"How about Hagan, Paul and Robert?"

"That's the scumbag who killed Ethan's mother. I don't remember the first name, but they weren't from around here."

"Paul was the guy who murdered his mother. His son Robert moved down here right before your brother did."

"Really? What a coincidence."

"Could be, but Robert was murdered."

There was ten seconds of silence before DeBlasi said, "Don't tell me you think Ethan had something to do with it."

"I've got my suspicions, but nothing more at this point. Getting back to Shaun Parker, did Ethan know him?"

"I don't know if there was a Shaun Parker."

"Ethan was in a bad accident. Do you know the name of the driver who hit him?"

"Oh boy, you're asking me to reach back. That was about twenty years ago. I don't know, and frankly, I don't even know if I ever knew the guy's name. All I knew was whoever hit him was drunk and got arrested."

"Where did the accident occur?"

"Tiny town called Greenville, outside of Appleton."

"You remember when it happened?"

"October 2001, right before Halloween."

46

———

When Vargas updated Sheriff Chester about the change in Hagan's time of death, he instructed us to bring Hannah in for questioning.

While we waited on her arrival, I put another call into the Greenville police department.

"This is Detective Luca with the Collier County Sheriff's Office, in Florida. I need information about a DUI crash. You have a DUI patrol, Sergeant?"

"No, sir. We've only got a dozen officers here. When did you say the DUI occurred?"

"Back in 2001. Late October, the days before Halloween, between the twenty-sixth and thirtieth of October 2001."

"That's a long while ago. I only started in 2007 myself. Hold on a minute. Let me ask the chief; he's been here forever."

I searched back issues of a newspaper, *The Post Crescent*, for articles on the crash Ethan Dwyer claimed he was in. A voice barked through the receiver.

"This is Chief Lasster. Who's this?"

"Chief, I'm Detective Luca, Homicide, Collier County Sheriff's Office."

"Homicide?"

"Yes, sir. I'm looking into an old DUI car crash from October 2001 involving a person of interest, Ethan Dwyer. I realize it's ancient, but I'm looking to identify the driver under the influence."

"It's fuzzy to me, were there any fatalities in the crash?"

"No, but I understand Ethan Dwyer was badly hurt and the drunk driver arrested."

"If there was an arrest I can look it up. You wanna hang on, or you want me to call you back?"

"If it's okay with you, I'll hang on."

"You said it was late October 2001, right?"

"Yes. I really appreciate this."

I sent a text to Vargas. She was in court, getting ready to go on the stand. I let her know I was waiting to hear if the driver who crashed into Dwyer happened to be one of the victims. I was reading a text from her when the chief got back on the phone,

"Detective Luca?"

"Yeah, I'm here."

"I remember this one now. I responded to the scene."

"Who was the driver of the other vehicle? The guy who was drunk?"

"Jeremy Kelly."

"Kelly? You sure?"

"Yep."

"I understand this wasn't this guy's first DUI."

"Yeah, habitual offender. I always thought he'd kill himself or someone else in a crash, but he was shot dead about ten years ago up in Appleton."

"He was murdered?"

"Yes."

"Did you find out who did it?"

"Kelly was from around here, but the homicide occurred in Appleton. Last I heard, they never caught the guy, but with everything going on, I lost track of the case."

"I'm familiar with case overload. I want to check on the proper spelling for Kelly. Is it double L Y, or does it have an E at the end?"

"K, E, L, L, Y. First name Jeremy."

After thanking the chief, I send a text to Vargas and got back on the phone.

"Homicide, Detective Harris."

"I'm Detective Luca, homicide, with the Collier County Sheriff's Office. I understand you have an unsolved by the name of Jeremy Kelly. Case is about ten years old."

"I'd have to check the cold case files. What's your interest in it?"

"It's a long story."

"Aren't they always."

"We've got a serial killer down here. A suspect we're following was badly injured by this Kelly in a DUI incident."

"So, it's a revenge hit, you think?"

"Could be, we have him linked to another revenge killing, but the evidence is thin. Can you check?"

"Hold on a sec, I'll jump into the cold case archive."

I heard him tapping away on a keyboard when he said, "Okay, here we go. Kelly, Jeremy, thirty-five-year-old Caucasian found washed up on Little Chute Island."

"Where's that located?"

"Fox River."

"What was the cause of death?"

"Looks like the guy drowned to death."

"Drowned? I thought he was shot to death."

"Cause of death is listed as drowning."

"Okay, but I'd like to look over the case file if that's all right with you."

"Sure, make a request through the portal, and I'll email it to you."

"Thanks. You're a prince for helping."

"Always happy to help a fellow officer. We got to stick together if we're gonna survive in today's world."

VARGAS WALKED through the door an hour later. "Hey Frank."

"How'd it go?"

"Good. Steinberg tried to get under my skin on cross, but he came across desperate. Trillo did a good job. It'll go to deliberations in a day, two at most."

"Be good to get that turd off the street."

"That's crazy that the guy who hit Dwyer was shot dead. You think it was Dwyer?"

"Yeah, well it seems the guy drowned to death."

"What? Your text said he was shot."

"The chief of that shit-ass town told me he was, but Appleton homicide said it was a drowning."

"Oh. Say, while waiting to testify, I was thinking we should get another opinion on the time of death."

"You don't trust Beasley?"

"No, it's not that. He's good but not infallible. It isn't an exact science, and with the politics, I think Chester will go for it."

"Good idea."

"You think so?"

"It's the right move. Maybe the DA could be helpful here. Explain how it could blow up in court and such."

"Yeah. Thume has Chester's ear."

"Nothing gets you run out of office like losing a big case."

Vargas stood. "Come on, let's go see them."

I had no interest in being reminded we were still grasping for answers. Getting in front of Chester about building a case on a suspect I had argued against going after was tough to stomach. A little white lie was the escape route I took.

"I'm waiting on a call from some guy who knew Dwyer and Hagan up in Wisconsin."

47

VARGAS HAD A FROWN ON THAT DIDN'T QUIET EXTINGUISH the glow from her skin. Confirming she was back to normal, she said, "You don't get up now, I'm going without you."

"I'm almost done. I got a couple left."

"See you later. I'll tell Chester you were too busy doing emails to see him."

I quickly read one more: a last warning concerning sensitivity training I had continually put off. It was a complete waste of our valuable time listening to people who never worked a day in the real world.

I followed Vargas out the door, leaving two emails unread: one from the Appleton Police Department, and an autopsy report on a high schooler who hung himself. There wasn't a doubt the poor kid took his own life, based on the scene and the background info we had developed. It was crazy to put the parents through one, but it was protocol.

Sheriff Chester was talking with DA Thume as we entered his office. Chester needed a haircut and had the slightest of stubble growth. He was a couple of years older than me but looked a lot older when not perfectly groomed, as he normally was.

Chester nodded but remained seated. "Detectives."

"Sir."

The DA shifted his chair over as Vargas and I sat.

Chester said, "Booth is playing hardball."

"After you called her to come in, DA Thume heard from Marcus Knight."

Thume said, "Knight advised me that Hannah Booth was refusing to come in voluntarily."

Vargas said, "Does she know about the change in Hagan's time of death? I didn't mention anything about it."

Chester said, "If someone leaked this, I'll turn this place upside down to find out who. I promise you, they'll never work again."

Thume said, "She's hiding something. Why else would she refuse to cooperate?"

I said, "Were we able to confirm the TOD change? Maybe someone in the coroner's office tipped Booth off."

Chester said, "I know Woller. He's a good man, and no way he leaked this. Woller believes the TOD is in a narrower range, well within the time frame for her to commit the homicide."

Vargas turned to Thume. "You going to issue an arrest warrant and force her in?"

Thume said, "Knight said he would organize a protest and televise it. He promised a turnout in the hundreds."

Chester said, "We've got to be careful. It's borderline, evidence wise. We arrest her, and she lawyers up—we learn nothing."

"Then we'd have to file charges based upon what we have, or drop it for the time being."

Chester said, "I need the two of you to nail the time line,

support it with witnesses and CCTV footage. We take this to a grand jury; we have to be on sound footing."

I said, "We'll do our best, sir."

"It's gotta be ASAP. There hasn't been a body in a couple of weeks, but the surveillance we have on her may have to stop. Knight said he was in touch with the American Civil Liberties Union and was going to file an invasion of privacy suit."

I shook my head. "Maybe we can drop back, observe her from a distance."

"I already instructed Gilby to pull back, cut their visibility."

"You may want to consider dropping the daytime surveillance, pick her up at dusk."

"I'll consider it. Meanwhile, it's time to get to work."

***

THE SUN WAS BLAZING through the window. Angling the blinds, I said, "We need to map every possible route from Hannah's house to where she was picked up in Lee. We don't even know where the hell Hagan got dumped in the water, but I'll bet it's either Clam Pass or Wiggins again."

"I'll check with the National Oceanography people, see if they can determine where it might be since he ended up in Pelican Bay."

"Good. Check with the marine department at Gulf Coast U. They know the tidal stuff and flow better than the Feds."

"I'm going to go over the whole thing about Hannah's son's death, talk to the Smyrna detective who thought it was suspicious."

Looking through the case file for the detective's name, I

said, "You wanna go downtown tonight? There's a jazz band at Cambier. We can grab dinner."

"Sounds nice. It's not supposed to rain, is it?"

"Nope."

I grabbed the phone and called Georgia. Put on hold, I went through my emails. The teen's autopsy report found no drugs, alcohol, or anything suspicious. A snake circled in my stomach at the thought of this fifteen-year-old believing things were so bad that he took his life.

Clicking up the case file from Appleton, Wisconsin, I skimmed the crime scene report and slammed down the phone. "Holy shit! This fucking Kelly guy was shot."

On the phone, Vargas waved me off.

"Hang up, Vargas. Get off the phone—this changes everything."

I kept reading as she finished her call.

"What are you so worked up about?"

"The driver who hit Dwyer, he was shot twice and dumped in the water. Sound familiar?"

"Oh my God. When was that?"

"About ten years ago. It's Dwyer's MO. This ain't no coincidence. This is Dwyer taking revenge—it's got to be."

Vargas came around my desk and looked over my shoulder. "What evidence do they have from the scene?"

"Not much. Holy shit, they recovered a shell!"

"Dwyer's been careful to pick up the shells."

"Maybe this was his first and he panicked."

"Could be. Send me a copy. My back's gonna go out reading over your shoulder."

We printed hard copies and pored over them.

The lead detective was a guy named Gunther Hendersen, and his summary read like surrender to me.

No arrests had been made, and they never identified a

strong suspect. After vetting the alibi of a man Kelly had a running feud with and getting a zero from the informant community, Appleton stopped looking. As far as they were concerned, the case was ice-cold a mere four months after Kelly was shot.

The autopsy concluded that death occurred from drowning, even though the reason Kelly drowned was because he was shot. If he wasn't in the water, he would have bled to death from the gunshot wounds.

A shell had two partial fingerprints but no match in Wisconsin's database. The fingerprints looked grainy, making me wonder how good their forensics were.

There was a witness, a Bill Dorough, who was fishing offshore, close to where the killing happened. He didn't see the killing, but when he heard the gunshot, he shined a light in the direction and saw a male run off.

He must have spooked the shooter, forcing him to leave before picking up both shells. It had to be.

"Vargas, we need to get our hands on the bullet fragments and that shell, fast."

"Why not call this Hendersen? Maybe he'll cooperate."

"He probably will if we don't show him up, but I can't deal with the frigging bureaucracy. It'll take two months. I'm gonna call Haines, see what he can do."

"Haines?"

"What's the matter?"

"Uh, you don't like him to start with, and you were concerned he'd take the case away."

"Nah, Haines is okay. He's actually a good guy when you get to know him."

Vargas raised her eyebrows and smiled.

"What's the matter, Vargas?"

"Nothing. Go ahead, call him."

48

―――――

In the two days since I'd sent Haines a digitized version of the fingerprints from Dwyer's water bottle and both ballistics reports, we made good progress on Hannah Booth.

The National Oceanographic Department was hesitant to state whether the Hagan corpse had floated south from Wiggins or north from Clam Pass, but Gulf Coast University had been steadfast in their belief that the body came down from Wiggins. That would mean that two bodies were dumped in Wiggins. That didn't jibe with the killer's MO—using different locations for each body. Were there two killers? Or was Hannah getting lazy? Or maybe it had to do with her bad back?

Vargas uncovered what I considered damning evidence: red-light traffic video of Hanna's car on Vanderbilt Drive. You couldn't see her face, but her blond hair was visible, and there was no doubt it was her.

Hannah was just several hundred yards from Wiggins Pass, and the time stamp was 7:09 p.m. There was a huge hole in the middle, but the jigsaw puzzle was filling up.

My pee-pee alarm buzzed, and like a five-year-old, I got up, marching to the bathroom. I was sitting on the throne, pressing my abdomen in an attempt to coax a leak out when my phone vibrated. It was Haines.

"Hey, how you doing?"

"Good, Frank. The boys up in Green Bay think we've got a match."

"Fingerprints or ballistics?"

"Ballistics. They believe there's no doubt the gun used in the last killings is the same one used on Kelly."

"Wow. Unbelievable. What about the prints?"

"There were only partials on the shell, but they could be Dwyer's."

"How so?"

"They found eight matching points. Being partials, there just wasn't enough data to be conclusive."

Exhaling, I said, "Eight. The DA won't introduce it as evidence unless we have more than a dozen match points."

"I'm familiar. The bureau's guideline is a minimum of twelve to twenty. We get twenty, there is no witness the defense can put up to dispute it."

"What do you think of all of this?"

"It's early yet, you never know what else you'll learn."

He was hedging. I said, "So we got a good hand but not a full house?"

Haines laughed. "Kind of, but in reality, a seasoned prosecutor could make a good case out of this."

"I hope you're right."

"I'll send over the reports."

Bᴏʙ Wɪʟʟɪs ʜᴀᴅ ʀᴇᴛɪʀᴇᴅ after a thirty-five-year stint with the Tampa police department. In an attempt to fill his days and subsidize a passion for wine, Willis collected checks from defense attorneys to weigh in on fingerprint evidence. Even though he switched sides, I liked Willis; he was a witty bastard.

There was a new Cadillac SUV in the driveway of his Sarasota home. I rang the bell, and when Willis answered I pointed to the car. "The other side pays pretty good, huh?"

"That's my wife's, for her real estate business. Me? Only thing I care about in a car is if it starts."

"I'm with you. It's good to see you."

"Same here, my friend. Come in."

An open bottle of wine was sweating on the kitchen's white island. Willis opened a cabinet, grabbed a glass and poured a splash of vino in it. "See if you like it. It's a Portuguese white, an Alvarinho."

Bringing the glass up to my mouth, I remembered to look at the color and smell it first. It had a floral scent. I sipped it. "It's nice, light."

"Perfect for a late afternoon in the Sunshine State. Let's see the reports."

Willis opened the manila envelope, spread the papers apart, and took a magnifying glass out of a drawer. Hunched over, Willis moved the magnifier between the photos, consulting the FBI report as he did.

I poured myself another glass to keep from asking what he thought. It was good wine, and I wondered how much it cost while walking to the back window. Like a lot of places in Florida, there was a nice view—a corner of a lake with a preserve in the distance. I knew Sarasota was pricey, a bit cheaper than Naples, and guessed this one-story home was worth six hundred thousand.

The clink from setting down the magnifying glass made me turn around. Willis was pouring the last of the bottle into his glass. "This can go either way."

"I drove all the way up here for that?"

"Come here. I'll show you what we got." Positioning two of the photos together, he said, "These are the thumb prints." He pointed a pencil at the full print I'd lifted from Dwyer's water bottle. "Here we have a good tell, a bifurcation in the ridge line pointing down and here pointing up. That's two solid match points."

That sounded promising; what was the problem?

"And here we've got two very short ridges or dots. Again, almost an exact match, giving us four strong matches. Then we have these two swirls that are decent. Over here, the matches are slightly weaker, but it could be argued the pressure applied, perspiration, body oils, etcetera. Those are the things that get me the big bucks from defendants, but it can work against you. If you include them, you've got eight matches out of a about half a print."

"That's pretty good."

"Yes, but it doesn't meet most prosecutor's thresholds, and guys like us are paid to blow things up."

"What about the other print, the forefinger?"

"I was saving the bad news for last."

"You kidding me?"

"Wish I was, Frankie boy. There's not much that does match. I could sell a couple of them, but if I was you I'd look to exclude this."

"It's not the same person?"

"I don't see it."

"But the thumb print is?"

"There may not be enough for a courtroom, but I'd say ninety, ninety-five of a hundred it would be the same person."

49

"You want to go to Chester with this, Frank?"

"Chester? What's he gonna do for us? He hasn't worked a homicide in ten years."

"I thought he may be able make a suggestion, see something we don't because we're too close to it."

She had a point, but going to the sheriff would make me look like a rookie. "We can do this without him. Let's take our time and go over this again."

"But we've been over it already."

"Humor me, will you?"

"Okay, okay."

"On Hannah Booth, we've got the gun in her office, her hair on a corpse, and her alibi for the Hagan murder is shaky at best."

"That DUI seemed to clear things up, but all it did was keep us off her track."

"Maybe. But because of it, we can place her close to where we believe Hagan was dumped."

"She works at the church with each of the victims, and we know she argued with some of them."

"I'm not a fan of hers, but I just can't see her doing these killings."

"Because she's a woman?"

I shrugged. "I guess so."

"I'll let that slide, Frank, since you have bias training to do."

"No, it's not that. I mean, she's pretty big physically, but if she had to push one of these guys around or move a body—"

"A, she had a gun in her hand, and B, there was no evidence any of the bodies were dragged."

"All right, she's a strong suspect, but what's the motive?"

"Maybe she's nuts."

My pee-pee alarm sounded, and I hit snooze. "She seems pretty damn sane to me. Now, Dwyer. The guy who smashed into him is dead, along with the guy who killed his mother. That's a shitload of motivation."

"No doubt. But first off, Bobby Hagan was the son of the creep who killed his mother, and the time line is all wrong. Dwyer waits years to kill the drunk who hit him, and then decades to kill the son of the guy who killed his mother? It doesn't make sense."

"The way you say that almost makes me forget we have what looks like his print on a shell."

"It's a partial, Frank. And you're forgetting the other print that's no match."

"It's a partial, Vargas."

Vargas sighed. "What am I gonna do with you, Frank?"

I lowered my voice. "I have a couple of ideas."

She smiled. "If you're a good boy, maybe later."

I gave her a thumbs-up. "I promise."

"Back to business. Hannah Booth seems a lot stronger than Dwyer. This whole thing with the drunk driver killing, I don't want to take a shot at anybody, but the guys up in Appleton might not have the tools nor the time to track down who killed him. Don't get hung up on him, Frank."

She could be right, but my gut had a heavy leaning toward Dwyer. Were my instincts failing me again? Last night, Mary Ann said I was hung up on the types of movies we watched. I liked to watch shows that were realistic. How could people watch all that fantasy stuff? It was silly. It was a preference, not a hang-up. She also said, and not for the first time, that I was hung up on the types of food I ate. I hated Indian and Chinese food, that's all.

Hang-ups. Was I hung up on Dwyer? My reminder to go to the bathroom sounded. I got up. Sitting on the throne I did some of my best thinking. "I gotta go to the boy's room." I sat on the bowl, thinking it'd been almost two years since cancer changed my urinating ritual. Early on, it was weird sitting like a girl, but it ended up being another lesson in how adaptable humans can be. My doctors taught me how to apply pressure using my abdominal muscles, and I used the tactic. About ten minutes later, my makeshift bladder slowly but surely released a trickle that turned into a stream.

Pressure. If there was something to release, pressure would ultimately get it out, I thought as I zipped up.

Washing up, I was taken aback by my image. I stepped back a bit, hoping it was the light, but I still looked tired and older than my forty-two years. No one had given me the George Clooney look-alike thing in a while, and there was no reason to. I ran a hand through my hair, forcing my attention back to the killings.

Swinging the door open, I announced, "Vargas, we're gonna bring both of them in. Apply pressure and see what breaks."

"But they'll have lawyers with them."

"Probably. Way I see it, we lay it on, and see their reaction when we tell 'em we got them."

"I donno, Frank. I can't see it working."

"People lie to us all the damn time. There's no law saying we can't do the same."

"If they take the fifth, then what?"

"We learn what they're afraid of. If someone didn't do something they won't hide behind the fifth."

"That's not always true, Frank."

"I don't care about any other case but this one right now. We've got two pieces of indictable infor—"

"Incriminating, not indictable."

"Okay, okay. Geez, we on the same side or what?"

Vargas shook her head. "You done?"

I shrugged.

"Good. Let's get back to grunting this, as you like to say."

"Okay, did you check to see if there was any record of Dwyer having a SunPass or E-ZPass?"

"I put out the requests, like you asked, including the airlines who operated between Fort Myers and Green Bay around the time the murder took place. It's a moon shot."

"Good, good. What about any video footage? Ten years ago, there were hardly any cameras around. But maybe in a canvas of the area where the murder occurred, there might be something like a school, a bank, or maybe an ATM."

"Did they even have ATMs ten years ago? Anyway, I made the request to Appleton and Green Bay to see what might be out there. This Detective Donofrio—he was really helpful, said he'd normally dismiss the request based on how long ago it was, but he promised to look into it."

"If you called me, I'd go out of my way too."

"What's that supposed to mean?"

"You girls got an advantage, that's all."

She put her hands on her hips. "Only with cavemen like you, Frank."

"Lighten up. Really. You got to relax, Vargas."

"And you've got to zip it. Okay?"

I made the T sign with my hands, "Okay, time out. How long is it going to be before they get back to you?"

"Everybody knows this is hot."

50

———

Vargas and I looked at the video feed of the interview room. Dwyer was wearing a pair of black wire-frame glasses. It was the first time I'd seen him wear glasses. Between the way his hair was parted and the spectacles, he was going for the Johnny Depp look. Dwyer seemed calm, playing with his cell phone despite the red lettered sign prohibiting cell phone usage.

Vargas shook her head. "I still can't believe he came down without a lawyer."

"Plays in our favor if he's overconfident."

"Maybe he's just innocent."

"This guy thinks he's smarter than everyone, and he may be, but I've locked up a few geniuses over the years."

"Do I have to lower the air?"

Smiling, I nodded.

"You're so predictable, Frank."

Vargas headed to the thermostat as I said, "I got my ways of doing things."

It wasn't superstition—making a suspect feel they had no control—it was something I learned at John Jay College.

Dwyer slowly shifted toward the door as we entered.

I said, "Hello, Mr. Dwyer."

He nodded.

"Are the glasses new?"

"Not really."

Vargas hit record, recited the formalities, and said, "Mr. Dwyer, you have the right to be represented by an attorney. If you are unable to afford counsel, the court will appoint a lawyer at no cost to you."

"I'm well aware of my rights."

"You're declining the right to have an attorney present at this interview?"

"Yes. I've nothing to hide."

Ah, the profession of innocence. It came early, a good sign.

Vargas said, "Before we get started, I'd like to thank you for coming in voluntarily."

Dwyer raised his eyebrows. "I wouldn't call it voluntary. Detective Luca said I'd be arrested if I didn't appear."

"I never said that."

"Not exactly, but you certainly inferred it."

Vargas said, "You're here now, so let's get to it. Shall we?"

Dwyer shrugged.

I said, "Would you consider yourself a patient man?"

"Patient? Yes, I believe I am. Hebrews 10:36 teaches us, 'You need to be patient to do the will of God and receive what he promises.'"

"So, having to wait ten years to get revenge for the murder of your mother wasn't difficult?"

"Detective Luca, the serpent who killed my mother is in jail."

"And to get at him you went after his son, Robert Hagan."

Dwyer shook his head. "You're envisioning connections that don't exist."

"It's a coincidence, is it, that the son of the man who tortured and murdered your mother was killed? A man who you knew and followed down to Florida."

Dwyer grimaced as he stretched his back. "We've gone over this before. I have nothing further to add."

Vargas said, "Back bothering you?"

"Never goes away."

I asked, "Is it another coincidence that Jeremy Kelly, the drunk who crashed into you, inflicting injuries so bad you had to learn to walk again, was found shot to death?"

"I heard he died, but that was years after the accident."

"With Kelly's record, I wouldn't call that an accident, I'd say it was an eventuality."

Vargas said, "You must have been livid at Kelly."

"Of course, I was upset, but that doesn't mean I killed him."

"Were you in Wisconsin on the day Kelly was found shot?"

"No."

"Are you certain?"

"Yes. I was here, living in Florida."

"Do you own a Glock .44?"

"No."

"Have you ever owned one?"

"No."

"How would you explain the fact that the bullets found in Kelly's body match those found in Bobby Hagan and Shaun Parker?"

Dwyer blinked, pulled his glasses off and rubbed his right eye. Was there something there, or was it just an errant eyelash?

"I wouldn't have a clue."

"Maybe you can tell us how your fingerprint got onto the .44 shell found at the scene."

"My fingerprints? It's apparent you're fishing, Detective."

"We're not. It's true. Your fingerprint was found on a shell left by the Glock that killed Jeremy Kelly."

"That's impossible. I wasn't there. I was in Florida."

"Tell me if this sounds possible. As a patient man, you waited years before taking action, even moving to Florida, before getting your revenge. I got to hand it to you. It was good planning, but we've got you now."

Dwyer's eyes flicked between Vargas and me before he said, "If you had proof you would have arrested me. This interview is over."

He was right, whether for the time being or not was the question. The answer was going to have to wait, because Hannah Booth was coming for an interview in an hour.

LIPS PURSED, Hannah Booth towered over her attorney as they made their way to the interview room Dwyer had vacated. The fear of never leaving the building when people came 'downtown' always threw people off. The vulnerability Hannah displayed proved she wasn't immune.

It was my first encounter with Marcus Knight, who was one of those annoying people who never fully lifted their feet when walking. The irritating, scuffling sound put Knight squarely in my dislike column. Hannah offered a soft hello, but Knight only nodded as they walked through the door I held open.

I got another whiff of Hannah's fruity perfume as Vargas and I sat on the opposite side of the stainless-steel table. I liked it, wondering how it'd smell on Mary Ann as she handled the formalities.

"I'd like the record to reflect that my client, Hannah Booth, has come voluntarily, at considerable inconvenience and expense."

Most expensive services never mentioned price, but there were those at the top of every field who wore the high fees they charged like a badge. I'm sure it helped to convince many they were the best. I said, "Duly noted."

Vargas said, "Mrs. Booth, thank you for coming today. We have several questions that will help to clarify what role, if any, you had in—"

"My client denies having a role in any crime."

Since I didn't want to antagonize the pompous jerk, I didn't tell him Vargas hadn't even finished the role reference. Instead, I said, "Mrs. Booth, where were you between the hours of four p.m. and eight p.m. On August twentieth?"

Hannah's blond hair swayed from her ear as she tilted her head. "August twentieth? I really don't remember."

"Would it help to remind you that August twentieth was the night you were arrested for driving under the influence?"

A rosy hue rushed over her cheeks. "Oh. I was working at the church until sometime after six thirty or so."

"You sure about that? The Lee County arrest records state you were pulled over at seven forty p.m."

"No, I'm pretty certain I was there until at least six thirty."

"Was anyone with you at the church?"

"Uhm, there may have been, but I was in my office."

"Were you drinking alcohol in the church?"

"No, of course not. Minister Booth doesn't permit alcohol on the premises."

"When you left, where did you go?"

She reached for her lower back, "It was a very stressful day, and my husband was up in Immokalee. He wouldn't be home until ten or so, so I went for a drive to clear my head."

"Were you drinking and driving?"

Knight put his hand on Hannah's arm and said, "Mrs. Booth was charged and accepted responsibility for her actions that night."

I said, "I'm simply asking whether she was drinking as she drove."

"No, I'd never do that."

"If you weren't drinking at work or behind the wheel, how do you explain your point two seven alcohol blood level at the time of arrest?"

Knight leaned over and whispered in her ear. Hannah said, "On the recommendation of counsel, I am taking the fifth."

I slammed a palm onto the table. "The fifth? Were you drinking or not?"

"Mrs. Booth has already invoked her legal right. Next question."

Vargas nudged me under the table and said, "You had a bad day and left your office to take a ride and clear your head. I get it. Many times I do the same thing. Where did you drive to?"

"Just around, you know. I remember driving on Livingston for a while, and then I was in Bonita."

"Were you in the Wiggins Pass area that night?"

She answered too quickly. "No."

Vargas opened her file and slid the time-stamped photo of her on Vanderbilt Drive and Wiggins. "How do you explain this?"

She didn't touch the photo, but Hannah's blue eyes moistened. "I—I, uh, I donno. Maybe I was wrong."

Knight said, "Mrs. Booth's memory was impaired that evening."

I said, "She was over the legal limit but far from the blackout zone."

Knight said, "Alcohol effects have been known to vary dramatically from person to person."

"There's a significant period of time and events that need explanation."

"My client has already said she does not recall."

"We'll see how a jury likes that."

"If you're threatening an arrest, this interview and our cooperation are over. Is that understood?"

Vargas said, "We're trying to piece together a time line for Mrs. Booth on August twentieth."

"And we're attempting to cooperate."

I said, "Okay, let's move on. As you know, we found Mrs. Booth's hair on Shaun Parker's body and the gun used in three killings in her office. We've heard the denials regarding them, but forensics has discovered her DNA on Dick Cornwall's body."

The color drained out of Knight's face so fast he looked like an outline in a coloring book. Hannah scrunched up her face and said, "What?"

Knight said, "Take the fifth, Mrs. Booth."

Hannah said, "I don't understand. How they could have found that?"

"We'll find out what they have in discovery."

"But isn't that after an arrest?"

"Yes, but don't concern yourself about that."

"But I can't get arrested. No, I didn't do anything. I swear."

Knight rose. "I'm afraid this interview is over, detectives.

You've upset my client and we're leaving." He grabbed Hannah's elbow and headed out the door.

When the door slammed shut I said, "We got something here."

"I don't know if it was so smart to lie about the DNA, Frank."

Smiling, I said, "Her denial seemed genuine, but there was no doubt she's guilty of something."

I turned my cell on as Vargas said, "That was bizarre."

"Yeah, and that bullshit about her not remembering. Where was she? She lied about being close to where Hagan's body was dumped."

"You know what it means if she was telling the truth about Cornwall?"

I nodded. "We're dealing with two killers."

"I doubt it, though. She's been deceptive from day one."

"Shit, a voice mail from Minister Booth. Probably wants to piss on me for bringing his wife in again. Since you had a hand in this, you should get reamed as well." I put the speaker on and hit play:

"Detective Luca. This is Minister Booth, please get down here as soon as possible. I found something disturbing, and please don't say anything to Hannah, okay? Just get here as quickly as possible."

51

Hands jammed in his pockets, Minister Booth walked over as I pulled into the parking lot.

"Thank you for coming so quickly, Detective."

I shook his clammy hand. "No problem, Minister. What's going on?"

"Follow me, but please keep things quiet."

Booth walked through the doors of the church and down the nave's center aisle. Empty churches were places many took solace in, but they made me uncomfortable. Was it the thought of being alone with God or the possibility I'd have to examine myself?

I followed Booth up a step to the altar area. He hit a switch and the lights in an area behind a screen lit up. "It's in the chancel." We took another step up and around the screen. The space was dominated by a wooden buffet topped with a white lace runner. Anchoring the table was a large Bible, resting open, in a brass stand.

"I was getting prepared for Sunday's services and noticed the runner was dirty." He pointed to a gray smudge. "I went to grab a clean one in here." Booth grabbed a knob and pulled a door open, revealing a six-inch-high stack of linens.

"It's behind the runners."

I pulled on gloves and bent down. What was in there? A body part? Money?

"When I saw it I didn't do anything. I never touched it. It sickened me having it so close to the altar."

I reached behind the linens. It was a gun, a black Glock .44.

Recovering my balance, I snapped three pictures of the gun before removing and bagging it.

"Any idea who might have hidden it here?"

"No. It's shocking. I can't imagine."

"Who has access to this area?"

"It's reserved for clergy, but as you can see, it's accessible to anyone."

"You were concerned about mentioning your call to Hannah. Why was that?"

Booth swallowed. "Well, I don't think she has anything to do with it, but if she does, well, she'll have to answer for it."

"I appreciate your neutrality, Minister. You're an honorable man. I'm going to ask you to keep this quiet until we can figure out if it's related to the homicides."

Booth nodded. "I understand. I hope the truth comes out quickly. Under the present circumstances, I'm very uncomfortable and will be praying that my wife has nothing to do with all this. If she did . . ." He spread his arms out. "All of this will be lost. We'll have to shut down, I'm sure."

"We can test and analyze within hours. You won't have to wait long."

"I can't bear to think she . . . she was involved in anything like this, and I missed it."

I patted his shoulder. "Don't take this the wrong way, but I've come to realize we never really know somebody."

"God knows. He knows every hair on your head."

I tucked the bagged Glock in my jacket, and Booth walked me out. Saying goodbye, I couldn't imagine what he was going through. His closest confidant, his wife, had possibly betrayed everything he stood for. I wanted to peel out of the lot but couldn't alarm Booth any further, so I took my time pulling out and called Vargas.

***

"You know, Vargas, in my twenty years of law enforcement, I've only witnessed five ballistics tests, but here we are, back in the basement in the space of a couple of months."

"This is my third, and with that musty smell I hope it's my last."

I leaned into her, putting my hand on her butt. "You smell nice, like Dove soap."

Vargas elbowed me, whispering, "Knock it off, Frank." The ballistics tech came back in announcing he was ready.

I handed a pair of ear protection muffs to Vargas and put on a pair myself. The tech inserted the Glock into the funnel, looked at us, and pulled the trigger. The bullet streaked through the water, reminding me of a submarine's torpedo from a War World II movie. We removed our ear protection as the tech scooped the bullet out of the tank.

"Let me see that."

The tech bagged the bullet and handed it to me. There didn't appear to be anything remarkable, but the testing to come could elevate the slug's reputation to extraordinary. Handing the bag back, we followed the tech to the forensics lab upstairs.

I sat on one of the lab's stainless-steel stools staring at the back of a tech hunched over a microscope. Vargas had left to grab us coffee. I got up and began pacing the room, which was at least ten degrees too cold for me.

"Biting your fingernails?"

Taking a coffee from Vargas, I said, "Uh, had a hangnail."

"Calm down. We'll get the results when they're ready."

52

———

A STREAK OF ORANGE BURST ONTO THE HORIZON. MY WATCH read 6:39 a.m. Eight officers were strategically positioned, watching the house. The ultimate plan had us apprehending the suspect leaving the house before 7 a.m. The backup, which looked likely, was to have a plainclothes officer knock on the door.

There was only one light on in the house as I gave the order to pull back out of the front door's sight line. In the eight minutes it took to hit 7:00 a.m., daylight had poured in. I gave the signal. The youngest member of our team walked up to the front door and rang the bell.

A light came on in the foyer a second before the front door opened. As instructed, the officer told the suspect that his car was on fire. When the suspect stepped out of the house, three officers, guns drawn, rushed from the side of the house.

I trotted over. "You're under arrest for the murder of Robert Hagan." Reciting the Miranda warning, I felt a pair of icy eyes boring into me as the cuffs were snapped on.

An officer put the accused in the back seat of a patrol car, and in less than five minutes from my order, the suspect was on the way to the station.

THE DA HAD some concerns with the circumstantial aspects of the case. They believed a jury would understand the threads of evidence and vote to convict, but there was uncertainty. Attempting to mitigate the risk, the suspect was charged with three more counts of murder and would face the death penalty. The hope was to force a plea of guilty in exchange for dropping the capital punishment.

Vargas and I drove alongside the jail's twelve-foot-high fence and pulled into the parking lot. Walking up the entryway, Vargas pointed to a car waiting to exit. "That's Minister Booth leaving."

"He's a good guy. It's a shame he's gotten pulled into all this."

We slid our IDs under the glass, and the guard buzzed us in. After signing in and dropping our weapons, we were buzzed through another gate and headed to the jail's interview room.

"I prefer being on my own turf, Vargas."

"Maybe, but you can't argue with the desperation someone feels being behind bars."

Waiting to be let through another door, I said, "You're right. But that room makes me claustrophobic."

"You'll survive, Frank."

"Ha-ha. So, what do you think our chances are of getting a plea?"

"Fifty-fifty."

The door clanged shut behind us. A guard escorted us down a dark corridor lined with steel doors whose four-inch-square windows threw columns of light into the hallway. The muffled sound of someone singing was interspersed with an inmate banging a door with a tray. You couldn't put a piece of paper between Vargas's shoulder and mine.

The guard punched a code into a keypad, opening a door to a cinder-block square whose size reminded me to take deep breaths. Four chairs, whose white plastic had gone charcoal, were set around a metal table bolted to the floor.

The door slammed shut. I took the chair closest to the door, concentrating on my breathing as Vargas blabbed about the upcoming weekend. The door's locking mechanism whirled, and the door opened.

A zebra-patterned jumpsuit hung tent-like off Dwyer's shoulders. Dwyer offered his cuffed hands to the guard. I said, "It's okay. Take 'em off."

Dwyer pushed up his glasses before rubbing his wrists. He looked me in the eye, gently lowered himself into the chair opposite Vargas, and said, "I knew you'd be here before my lawyer said you'd be, asking me to cop a plea."

Vargas said, "It's in your best interest, Ethan."

"Oh, come now, Detective, you expect me to believe that? Why would the prosecutors offer any kind of deal?"

"A trial is a costly and lengthy process."

Dwyer smirked. "Yeah, right. The truth is, they're afraid to go up against me in court. They don't have anything concrete, just a series of unconnected strings."

Vargas said, "Don't forget this is a capital punishment case. You lose, and you're facing the death penalty."

I said, "Let's review," I finger quoted, and continued, "The strings, shall we?"

"This chair is hard as a rock. Isn't there anything more comfortable? I've got injuries, and they come with rights, even in prison."

"I'm with you on the chairs, but I'm afraid there's nothing we can do."

Vargas said, "If it'll help, feel free to get up, move around some."

"Thank you. Staying in motion does relieve some of my pain."

I said, "Let's get to it. You're correct that we've been authorized to explore a deal, but wrong if you think we don't have more than enough to get a conviction. For starters, we have your mobile phone records placing you in the vicinity of each of the Collier County killings near the times of death—"

"What possible motivation would I have to kill those poor men?"

"That's a good point."

Dwyer's smile crumpled when I said, "The DA is really good in a courtroom. Did I mention that he personally prosecutes every capital punishment case? Anyway, he'll paint you as a loser, hell-bent on revenge."

"Loser? Do you know I have an IQ of one forty-four?" Dwyer winced as he got up. "I'll bet the DA's no more than one oh five, one ten, at a maximum."

I looked at Vargas before saying, "The fact is, Bobby Hagan, the son of the man who killed your mother, was found shot dead. A man you knew and worked with at Booth's church, a man you followed down to Florida from Wisconsin."

"Pure coincidence. You can't prove that I followed him here."

"Maybe, but like I said, the DA is very convincing in a courtroom. Isn't that true, Vargas?"

"No doubt, he's one of the best I've ever worked with. I can't remember the last case he lost, if he did lose."

"It had to be before I got here, but either way, I know he's never lost a capital punishment case."

Dwyer put his palms on the table and leaned in. "This is a pathetic attempt to scare me. I'm intelligent. I don't allow my emotions to rule me. You have nothing on me."

I said, "That's what you think—that we came down here with nothing?"

Vargas said, "Maybe you should sit down, if you feel okay."

Dwyer eased himself into a chair. "All this manufactured drama—it's almost comical."

"Nothing funny about getting strapped onto a gurney and getting stuck with a dose of pentobarbital."

Vargas shuddered nicely.

"It'll never happen."

"You want to take the chance, that's your call. But I'll tell you, the DA said if they don't get the death penalty he was going to make sure you were also tried in Wisconsin."

"Wisconsin? On what?"

"Kelly, the guy you shot because he smashed into you."

"Really? How do propose proving that?"

"Pretty easily, actually. What we're going to tell you has not even been shared with the Green Bay police."

Vargas said, "The ballistics reports confirm that the gun used to kill Kelly and Hagan were one and the same."

"If I wanted to kill the drunk bastard I wouldn't wait ten years. Besides, I moved to Florida before it happened and never went back."

"I say you did. I say you drove up to Green Bay, killed Kelly, and drove back down."

Dwyer crossed his arms over his chest. "I believe that's called hearsay."

I reached into my breast pocket, pulled out a document,

and placed it on the table. "You were good, almost invisible, right, Vargas? Except you made a little mistake—you got a ticket for running a red light."

Dwyer picked up the photocopy of the ticket. "So what? This doesn't mean anything."

"It puts you in the same town. In fact, just a couple of streets away from where you shot Kelly, on the same day. Now, that's a heck of a coincidence for someone who lives in Florida."

"I have friends in Wisconsin. I went visiting, that's all."

"Why would you lie about it, then?"

"Because you can't trust the system. I tell the truth, and it will go the way the system wants it to. Nothing you can do."

Vargas said, "You know he's right, Frank. Look at all the times we work ourselves silly arresting some creep, only to have the court release him."

Dwyer smacked a palm on the table. "You see, there you go. The system is incapable of working. The piece of debris who raped and tortured my mother before killing her had just been released from prison. She didn't have to die. I was left alone, with nobody." He wrestled getting up. "Do you realize what it's like to be shuffled inside the foster care system? It's another disastrous system that doesn't work. You ask me, it's worse than having no system. The kids in it are better off on the damn streets."

Vargas said, "What a terrible thing for a child to have to endure. How old were you when this happened?"

"I had just turned eight." Dwyer shook his head. "My entire world was taken from me by that reprehensible thug. If the system operated properly, she'd be alive today." He wagged a finger and sat back down. "There's a certain subset of the population that is irredeemable. They'll never change, and there is absolutely no point in giving them second, third, and fourth chances."

I wanted to tell him I agreed, but Vargas was on a roll. She said, "It was shocking to see Paul Hagan's record. He should never have been allowed to walk the streets again." She reached across the table and put her hand on Dwyer's hand. "I'm so sorry you had to suffer through all that. I can't imagine how you dealt with such trauma."

Dwyer shrugged. "The void of losing your mother, especially in such a brutal attack, is a pain so deep, it's indescribable."

"You poor thing."

Dwyer's eyes glistened. "It took me years to recover from the emptiness. It never went away, but I started listening to God and could function."

"And then you are hit by a drunk driver. How tragic. How unfair, after what happened to you, to almost get killed in a crash and suffer such debilitating injuries."

Dwyer hung his head. "Let down by the system again."

"Kelly had several DUIs—"

I moved my hand to avoid the spit that flew out of Dwyer's mouth as he said, "That bastard should have been behind bars, no less be allowed to operate a motor vehicle."

"I know, it's crazy. How long were you hospitalized?"

"In excess of two months."

I said, "I can't imagine that. You must have been really bad. They're always looking to kick you out after a couple of days."

"They put two frigging steel rods in my back. The pain was so intense I was on morphine for two weeks. I had to learn to walk again. Rehab was murder. Kelly received what he deserved."

"It's hard to argue with that."

Vargas said, "You really got some tough breaks. It's so unfair. Look, I'm not condoning what you did, but I promise you the circumstances of what happened to you as a child will be considered in a plea arrangement."

Dwyer stiffened. "I didn't do anything. Purely out of curiosity, what would a hypothetical deal look like?"

"If you tell us everything, helping to close out all the cases, we've got some flexibility."

"Define flexibility."

"You'd save your own life. The DA will drop his insistence on a death sentence."

"What about parole?"

Vargas said, "While it's unlikely, we'd argue the trauma you suffered caused mental instability, and a judge could be inclined to remand you to an institution where release is possible after treatment."

"An institution is a whole lot better place than any jail, especially one up in Wisconsin, where the winters will make your back problems a lot worse."

Dwyer paused before saying, "All this is interesting, requiring consideration. Can you return tomorrow?"

"Sure," Vargas said. "Is there anything we can get for you?"

"A Bible. Make sure it's the New International Version."

"Okay. No problem. Anything else?"

"I'm extremely bored. Could you secure a couple of books to read?"

"Sure. What do you like?"

"Autobiographies are my favorite, but any biographies of almost anyone, excepting politicians or celebrities, will do."

"Consider it done. We'll see you tomorrow."

53

———

A DOZEN REPORTERS FOLLOWED US TO THE PRISON ENTRANCE. Someone had leaked that a plea offer was made to Dwyer. I pushed a mic away and slipped our IDs to the guard. Once inside, we surrendered our weapons and went through the metal detector, which buzzed when I went through. I'd forgotten my valise contained a video recorder in case Dwyer was ready to come clean.

The corridor was as scary as it'd been yesterday, but the interview room didn't cause my heart to race. We had business to do, and I was proud that I'd risen to the task.

Vargas laid down a Bible and three other books, whose sizes intimidated me.

"Put that away, Frank. It'll scare him."

"I'm just being optimistic."

"Put it back in your briefcase."

I tucked the video recorder away as the door whirled open.

Dwyer saw the books, smiled, and raised his cuffed arms to the guard. I nodded approval. Hands free, Dwyer picked up the Bible, opened it, and read aloud, "Lord, hear my voice in the morning. I set my prayers before you and hope. Wickedness is not accepted by you. The arrogant cannot stand before your eyes. You hate all wrongdoers. Lead me, O Lord, in your righteous ways." He closed the Bible. "The book of Psalms is my favorite. It reads like poetry."

Vargas said, "That was nice."

Dwyer picked up a book. "Nice. I read Nikola Tesla by Cheney but never his autobiography. This will be great. Ah, Leonardo da Vinci, that's a good one, and Toscanini. What an interesting choice. You surprised me, Detective."

"I'm glad you like them. I told the woman at Barnes and Noble to suggest books that a very intelligent person would like."

The picture of da Vinci on the cover caught my eye. He had this mysterious look that made me want to read it. I'd have to pick up a copy—it would be my read for the year.

Dwyer eased into a chair. "Thank you. I sincerely appreciate it."

Vargas said, "Did you have time to think over our offer?"

Dwyer nodded. "I still believe, if treated fairly, I would beat the charges. However, if you guarantee me an opportunity for parole or release from an institution, I'll agree."

Vargas said, "We spoke to the DA, and he believes a path is possible, but if the judge insists on a prison term, it's likely to be a life sentence."

I said, "Remember, without a plea you'll be facing a death sentence."

Vargas said, "Please, Ethan, don't make the wrong choice."

"My life is in God's hands. He has additional work for me to do. I can be his advocate wherever he sends me."

Vargas said, "You'll take the deal?"

"That's what God wants me to do."

Vargas gave me a dirty look as I pulled out the recording device.

"It's the right choice, Ethan. You won't regret it. We need to get this on record. It's a formality. Would you mind if we recorded this?"

"That's fine."

I turned the recorder on, and Vargas said, "In exchange for Ethan Dwyer's admission of guilt, the Office of the Collier County Prosecutor has agreed to drop its demand for capital punishment. In addition, they will consider the information offered by Ethan Dwyer and appeal to the court for leniency."

"That's all you're going to say?"

"Trust me, Ethan, I've handled a hundred pleas. That's standard language."

"It's too general."

"We cannot commit to anything further as we don't know what you are going to tell us today. That makes sense, doesn't it?"

"I don't know."

"Do you trust me, Ethan?"

"I do."

"Don't worry. It's the way it's done. Okay?"

"All right."

"Good. Now, tell us what happened with Bobby Hagan."

"I kept track of the Hagans—at first it was my own fear. As a kid I was so traumatized by what Paul Hagan did to my mother that I lived in terror, believing his son would come after me."

Out of the corner of my eye I saw Vargas shaking her head.

"As I got older, my fear subsided and morphed into wanting them to live in fear and to feel the pain of losing a loved one. I wanted revenge, but the kind I desired, the kind I wasn't ready for. As a consolation, I harassed them, making threatening calls, throwing rocks through their windows." He laughed. "Even put a bag of shit in their mailbox. It was childish, but it felt good. Anyway, when they moved it was like my purpose, my identity, was taken from me. I know it sounds irrational, but that's how I felt."

"It's not crazy, that's the trauma talking."

"Anyway, asking around, a neighbor told me where they relocated to. To be honest, my doctor had advised me numerous times, with my back problems, I should move south and that made the move easier. I probably used the weather as an excuse, but everything started to come together when I met Minister Booth."

"You met him by following Bobby Hagan?"

"Yes. It was easier than I thought. I was so hung up on them, I assumed they knew who I was, but Bobby Hagan had no clue. I didn't even have to use an alias. He was in the church's support program and made a mockery of it, stoking my anger. He never stopped his evil ways. The more I learned about him, the less I liked. Apparently, his mother felt the same way—she kicked him out of her house."

"You mentioned Minister Booth. What role did he play for you?"

"Minister Booth opened my eyes up to the limitations of God's patience with us. The very first sermon I heard him give was a total revelation. I still remember how he explained that God speaks to us, that we must listen and act on God's word. He made it clear we couldn't be bystanders; we had to earn our salvation. This was contrary to every-thing I had been taught about an all-loving and forgiving God."

It made me think of the message I received growing up—

about how being in fear of doing wrong had dissolved into a touchy-feely, free-for-all with no price.

Dwyer continued, "It made total sense to me. Those who did wrong would pay a price. No deathbed conversion would allow someone like Paul Hagan to get into heaven beside my mother. Over the next several months, what Minister Booth preached gave me a sense of courage to do what I knew had to be done."

"He was telling parishioners to exact as God's vigilantes?"

"No, no. That's the thing about him. He would always preach about forgiveness and helping your brothers and sisters, to give them second chances. But I wanted him to raise an army for God to get justice. I asked him about it once, but he said only God had the power to instruct, that he was just a conduit for the written word of God. I was disappointed, but then he quoted a Bible passage that struck me, something that I believe deep in my core. Exodus 22, 'If a thief is found breaking in and is struck so that he dies, there shall be no blood guilt for him.'"

Vargas said, "In other words, if someone is doing wrong you can act and be blameless?"

"Exactly. The only judgment anyone should care about it is by God."

"After your talk with Minister Booth, is that when you decided to seek revenge?"

"No, not immediately. Frankly, I knew what it meant intellectually, but despite what these people had done to me, it was a frightening prospect to realize."

"What happened?"

"I studied the Bible. There were numerous examples, like Romans 13:4, 'If thou do which is evil, be afraid; for he beareth not the sword in vain; for he is the minister of God, a revenger to execute wrath upon him that doeth evil.' Then I listened for God to speak to me. When he did, I began to do his work."

"Was the first Jeremy Kelly?"

"Yes. I realize it was a selfish pursuit, but it was my first. The geography and time that had passed gave me confidence I would be unnoticed and able to continue to purge evil."

Emotionless, Dwyer told us he rented a car, driving straight through to Indiana, where he paid cash for a motel room. He arrived in Green Bay the next day, shot Kelly dead, and was back in Florida two days later.

I said, "If not for the shell left behind and the red-light ticket, it was almost perfect."

Dwyer shook his head. "There was someone fishing out there. Can you believe it? You couldn't eat anything out of that river. When he shined the light my way, it made me nervous, running off with only one of the shells."

"How did it make you feel?"

"I'm not saying I wasn't petrified, but it was exhilarating. There was finally justice, and the world was better off with men like Kelly out of the picture. He was a waste of humanity."

"Why didn't you go after Hagan right away?"

"From the onset, I wanted to go after Hagan. But I couldn't show God it was just about me. I felt I had to remain unselfish, do his bidding. He was sending me to cleanse evil, and there was plenty under his roof at The Spirit of Fellowship Church."

"The motivation for killing Kelly and Hagan is clear, but what about the others?"

"They were evil personified. In James 1:41 we're instructed, 'Therefore, get rid of all moral filth and the evil that is so prevalent.'"

"How did you get along with Hannah Booth?"

"She actually thought like I did, that Minister Booth was too forgiving and wasted too many resources on people that would never change."

"You liked her but framed her?"

"I didn't like her personally. She was playing around on the minister. Hiding the gun in her office was a perfect way to teach her a lesson."

"Hannah Booth was unfaithful to her husband?"

"Yes. Ronnie Sales was the latest."

Vargas and I exchanged glances. Sales lived off Conners Boulevard, near enough to Wiggins Pass. No wonder she didn't want to tell us where she was the night of her DUI arrest.

"You placed her hair on Parker's body?"

He nodded. "I really wasn't attempting to frame her. I knew it would place the focus on her. It worked, didn't it?"

54

———————

Switching to a new blade did the job. My face was as smooth as it had been in a long time. Twenty minutes late, I sprayed a dose of the Chanel cologne Mary Ann got me and buttoned the shirt she'd given me on my birthday. Before starting the car, I sent a text that I was on my way.

Weaving my way through tables filled with tourists, I spotted Mary Ann seated at a table facing the Gulf. Sipping from a tulip-shaped glass, she saw me and smiled. I was off the hook. Kissing her, I ran my hand down her bare shoulder. It felt like silk. She had the smoothest skin on the planet.

"You started without me?"

"I wasn't going to mention you being late." She pointed to the beach. "Consider yourself lucky, I could sit here for hours."

"It's a perfect night with the perfect woman."

"You do something wrong, Frank?"

"Me? Never. Just appreciating what we got." I picked up the wine list. "After the hearing today, we need to celebrate when we can."

The wine list was short and overpriced. I ordered a Ketel One with cranberry and an order of chips and salsa.

"I know, it was weird today. I felt bad for Dwyer. He never had a chance to live a normal life."

"Don't go liberal on me now."

"No, it's true, Frank. He had his life ripped apart when he was just a little boy."

"I know, just kidding. But he's going where he belongs."

"I feel we kinda misled him."

"He's nuts but not insane. Dwyer got a life sentence, which he sure deserved."

"And in Florida, life is life. He'll never get out."

"Amen."

"I wish there was a way, you know, like reprogramming or something, to give him a second chance."

"You're watching too much sci-fi. But talking about second chances. You heard who it was that went into that burning building off Imperial?"

"The man who saved all those kids? Who was it?"

"That guy with all the tattoos, from Booth's church."

"The one who did all those stints in prison?"

"Yep. That guy Corbin is a heck of an advertisement for Minister Booth's second-chance program."

"And you said it was a waste of time."

"I was wrong—dead wrong."

"Again."

"Don't I get a second chance?"

She leaned in, brushed her lips across my cheek, and whispered, "You're gonna get more than that when we get home."

THE NEXT BOOK in this series is, A Cold, Hard Case. Find it in eBook, Paperback, and Audio.

I hope you enjoyed reading this book as much as I enjoyed writing it. If you did, I'd appreciate it if you would write a quick review on Amazon or your favorite book site. Reviews are an author's best friend and even a quick line or two is helpful. Thanks, Dan

OTHER BOOKS BY DAN

Complicit Witness

Push Back

Ambition Cliff

You can keep abreast of my writing and have access to books that are free of discounting by joining my newsletter. It normally is out once a month and also contains notes on self- esteem, motivational pieces and wine articles.

It's free. See bottom of my website: www.danpetrosini.com

ABOUT THE AUTHOR

Dan is a USA Today and Amazon best-selling author who wrote his first story at the age of ten and enjoys telling a story or joke.

Dan gets his story ideas by exploring the question; What if?

In almost every situation he finds himself in, Dan explores what if this or that happened? What if this person died or did something unusual or illegal?

Dan's non-stop mind spin provides him with plenty of material to weave into interesting stories.

A fan of books and films that have twists and are difficult to predict, Dan crafts his stories to prevent readers from guessing correctly. He writes every day, forcing the words out when necessary and has written over twenty-five novels to date.

It's not a matter of wanting to write, Dan simply has to.

Dan passionately believes people can realize their dreams if they focus and act, and he encourages just that.

His favorite saying is – "The price of discipline is always less than the cost of regret"

Dan reminds people to get the negativity out of their lives. He believes it is contagious and advises people to steer clear of negative people. He knows having a true, positive mind set makes it feel like life is rigged in your favor. When he gets off base, he tells himself, 'You can't have a good day with a bad attitude.'

Married with two daughters and a needy Maltese, Dan lives in Southwest Florida. A New York native, Dan has taught at local colleges, writes novels, and plays tenor saxophone in several jazz bands. He also drinks way too much wine and never, ever takes himself too seriously.

He puts out a twice-a-month newsletter featuring articles, his writing and special deals and steals.

Sign up at www.danpetrosini.com